T0278838

EUPHORIA DAYS

GREAT PLACE BOOKS

TRANSLATED FROM SPANISH BY LIZZIE DAVIS

EUPHORIA DAYS

PILAR FRAILE

AC/E

ACCIÓN CULTURAL
ESPAÑOLA

Support for the translation of this book was provided by Acción Cultural Española, AC/E.

PUBLISHED BY GREAT PLACE BOOKS
WWW.GREATPLACEBOOKS.COM
COPYRIGHT © 2024 PILAR FRAILE
ENGLISH TRANSLATION © 2024 LIZZIE DAVIS
ALL RIGHTS RESERVED

DESCRIPTION: FIRST EDITION
PUBLISHER NAME: GREAT PLACE BOOKS
CITY OF PUBLICATION: CHICAGO, ILLINOIS
AUTHOR: PILAR FRAILE
LCCN: 2024936709
ISBN: 978-1-950987-51-1
DESIGNED BY AIDAN FITZGERALD
GPB 03

"Perhaps we should even redefine sovereignty, in light of the epidemic. The sovereign is now the one with the data."

—Byung-Chul Han, trans. David Ownby

GROWTH

María

I blame everything on the damn worms. If they hadn't shown up, I'd still be a part of WhiteAngel, Roger would still be my match, and society as a whole would be better off.

It was only a dream. But for some reason I couldn't stop thinking about it. It bothered me that I couldn't work out the chain of events. I turned the images over again and again, but there was no way of telling if it was us, Roger and me, putting the worms in our mouths, feeling them thrash against our palates before we bit into them, or if we were the ones being eaten.

I tried to forget the whole thing. Roger kept saying it wasn't important, that it was "brain junk." "Like the data the equipment collects after running for hours and hours," he said. "You just have to reformat yourself."

I told him about it one Thursday. I remember perfectly because on Thursdays, we had our weekly sex appointment, but that day, because of the worms, we decided against intercourse and went for a walk in the city instead.

1

The end-of-autumn light was nice, and the streets looked immaculate. Everything seemed to square with our data. According to the index for "degree of satisfaction with surroundings," October is the most pleasant time of year in the city, in contrast with the summer months, during which ninety percent of those surveyed stated they'd like to be somewhere else and only ten percent are actually able to travel. Our objective was to always be bettering figures.

That's what Roger and I were working toward.

Big data for happiness. We'd been running thousands of databases for the better part of a year, and in that time, we'd developed seven new algorithms to manage them. We were WhiteAngel, and together, we were invincible.

That's what Manuela told us right when we transferred our first findings to the server. We got a message in seconds. Sometimes I wonder how she does it, she's the epitome of efficiency. Though I guess she doesn't have much choice. She's in charge of lots of teams, WhiteAngel and six others.

My message said: "Mary"—Manuela knows I think María sounds old-fashioned. Our old boss, Alois, was very considerate, too, but he was always forgetting those details that make the difference between a good boss and an exceptional one—"We're proud of you. This is a giant leap for mankind. Do you realize that? Now the whole world will be happier. WhiteAngel is invincible. If I were you, I might be too happy to sleep tonight. Hugs and kisses!"

Roger didn't let me read his. Of course, our agreement didn't say we had to tell each other everything, just keep our weekly sex appointment. It worked out to be about the same as taking antidepressants, but without any negative side effects.

Our profiles made it clear: we weren't looking for romantic partners. Our work was too important for distractions.

We were lucky our data was such a good fit. Otherwise, we would have had to find different matches for intercourse. And that would have meant setting up dates, comparing work schedules, making explanations every day—a satisfactory, regular sexual encounter requires a base level of mutual understanding and the exchange of personal information. Exhausting. Although it's true that we could have opted for more infrequent encounters, which require a minimal flow of information between participants. But then you have to do at least one search per week, a complete waste of time.

One week after our fall walk, we realized some of our early algorithms weren't compatible with the databases. In the end, we could only save four of the seven we had developed. We weren't starting over completely, but almost.

Our team morale wasn't great. In fact, it was probably almost as low as it had been those first few months, when we were still working hard to devise our first algorithm. We were worried we wouldn't make it past the trial period, that WhiteAngel would be the first of the teams to dissolve.

Nothing would have served us better that Thursday than our sex appointment. The walk the week before had confirmed our results were accurate: indeed, the city was pretty in the fall, the yellow of the sycamore leaves on the boulevards, the shop windows that lit up as night fell, in contrast with the purple sky, the brightly colored clothing—since no one wears dark colors in the fall anymore—it all made for a harmonious scene. But it hadn't increased our levels of dopamine and serotonin, which was the point.

I tried to convince myself that we really needed that session. But every time I thought about sex with Roger, the image of worms came to mind. There were a lot—millions, maybe—moving like a single organism, white or off-white. Very unpleasant, all of it.

Over the course of those eight days, I'd tried everything to get free of them: blocking them by envisioning something else—the wide-open countryside was usually a good choice—breathing deeply, filling up my abdomen, trying to get my mind to go blank, counting to one, two, three hundred, a thousand. Nothing. They wouldn't get out of my head.

I told Roger I wouldn't be able to, that I had a family meeting. I don't know why I lied to him. I had never done it before. I had made up my mind to tell him I didn't want to have sex that night, and when he looked at me with those super-blue eyes, I just couldn't admit that it was because of the dream.

I don't know what was worse: the image of the worms, which was really more a feeling than an image, like being devoured by tiny mouths (do worms have mouths?); the idea that I was devouring them, choking on their slime as it slid into my throat; or, that I had lied to Roger.

All three were very unpleasant.

Back at home, at my fake family meeting, I thought it might not be a bad idea to call my father. When I was about to dial his number, my head, as usual, started working on its own and imagined the conversation:

"How are you, Dad?"

"Oh, I'm fine. Just a little tied up with the latest orders."

My father owns a gift shop. It's an obsolete business, he maintains it at a loss, but there's no way he'll ever give it up. I've told him a thousand times it'd be more profitable for him to sell the shop and retire early than hold out and keep paying all the expenses. He gives me that faint smile he reserves for when I talk about the business. He started smiling that way after Mom died. Or maybe he smiled like that before, but I didn't realize it. Mom was such a big presence it's hard to say what Dad was like before she died.

"Oh, OK, I won't bother you then. I just wanted to see how you were."

"OK, sweetheart. But what about you? How is it at the top?"

When Dad uses that phrase, "at the top," I get the feeling he doesn't really mean it. There's, I don't know, a kind of undertone. Or maybe that's what his voice sounds like now that Mom is dead. The point is, as soon as I hear it, I stop wanting to tell him anything.

That's how I decided not to call Dad.

Things went from bad to worse after our second sexless Thursday. It turned out there was nothing wrong with our original algorithms. Our error lay in an incorrect scan of the previous data. That would have been a relatively easy fix, but by then, there was already more data available, and we couldn't just leave it out. It went against our principles. So we had to start from scratch.

Maybe we shouldn't have been discouraged, because these things happen with science, and our failure actually brought us much closer to truth than a false success, but Roger was crushed. I tried to convince him that we were just facing a new challenge and that we should be happy to do so, and he said I was right, my logic was impeccable, but I detected no enthusiasm in him. In fact, he stopped making jokes, which he hadn't stopped doing even in the early months, back when we had no idea what was going to happen.

Even though we were a team, when things got bad, Manuela would write to Roger. It didn't exactly bother me, but I think the failures, like the successes, belonged to us both. I'm sure, and I tell myself this so

I don't get upset, because that would be very irrational, that Manuela had a very compelling reason to write to him.

Roger didn't reveal the contents of her messages, and I briefly considered finding a way to hack into his account. I knew enough about him that I probably could. I knew that as a kid, he had a dog he adored, and they put him down the day before Roger turned fourteen. The dog's name was Buf, which is what Roger called him before he could talk.

I knew he really liked physics and that he used to dream of establishing a colony in Andromeda, like Thales of Miletus, one of his idols. But then he got older and stopped dreaming of becoming an astrophysicist and going to Andromeda, because the job market was bad, and besides, it wasn't a very realistic dream, so he went into pure mathematics instead. I'd have bet my right hand that his password was ThalesAndromeda_13. But hacking into his account would have been sinking pretty low, and even worse, it could have gotten me fired.

Manuela wasn't upset with us; it seemed we had nothing to worry about. She suggested we repeat the process and calmly proceed. You can't rush science.

Problem solved. Everything was fine. We would continue our search for the truth, to ensure greater happiness for all.

But Roger was still subdued. It was our fourth week without sex. The previous week, I had told him I couldn't because I had a dentist appointment, and it was clear Roger needed his endorphins and his dopamine and his oxytocin, so I went over to him. Normally we work at adjacent desks so we can check each other's progress without moving, but the last few days, he'd been at a table we put in front of the big window, in case a third member showed up.

When WhiteAngel was formed, Manuela had told us the team would eventually grow. The search for candidates had been ongoing. But when we started to bring in results, she decided we worked well enough on our own and didn't need anyone else.

I went over to the big window and said, "Roger." He didn't react. He seemed lost in the view of the city. He'd even sat down facing the window, not our tables, as we'd intended. That had annoyed me, but what could I do.

Since he wasn't saying anything, I gently touched his shoulder. His body felt hot. It was the same body I'd kissed and caressed in the months before. The same athletic build that had given me such pleasure. I couldn't figure out why it didn't appeal to me anymore. The human mind is a mystery. Fortunately, we're on the way to untangling it and putting an end to all the uncertainty.

He was a little startled. Like he was hypnotized by the traffic you could see through the window, out on the street. Those rows of red and white lights, like a flag in perpetual motion, looked pretty as the sunset.

"What's up?"

"Look, I've been thinking."

"Mmm."

"I can't figure out why I don't feel like keeping our sex appointments lately. Honestly, it's not you, you're an optimal lover."

Roger blushed a little when I said that, and I didn't understand why. It's true we had never verbalized our feelings toward each other as sexual partners, but I took for granted that we were a good fit. When the blushing went away, he looked at me questioningly, or maybe it wasn't a question in his eyes, it was hard for me to tell. In situations like that, I envy people who have a natural skill for interpreting facial expressions. Luckily, it won't be long before there's facial recognition software precise enough to ease all social encounters. Think of the misunderstandings we'll be able to avoid.

In the meantime, I had to categorize them myself. So I decided that, yes, Roger's look was questioning.

"I was thinking you might want to look for another match."

Roger's expression changed slightly. Was he surprised? Angry? What was I supposed to do, ask him? Isn't it impolite to ask someone if they're mad? Wouldn't that just make things worse? God, I was having such a hard time. I settled on surprise, because try as I might to evaluate, I found no logical reason for him to be angry. So, yes, it had to be surprise. Though I also couldn't figure out why he would be so surprised, but it seemed like a much gentler reaction, more appropriate to the circumstances. After all, I only had the good of the team in mind.

Roger, overcoming whatever emotion had him paralyzed, responded, "Another match?"

"Yes, at least until I feel better."

I didn't want to mention the worms again, because that would have meant explaining. It's not that I didn't want to explain, it's that I couldn't, because what would I have been bringing up, exactly?

My armpits started to sweat, and I was grateful I had put on twice as much deodorant as usual. Since I started dreaming about the worms, my body odor was more intense. I showered twice a day and put on extra body spray every morning, but even so, the odor would win out. It was very annoying.

I backed up a little so he wouldn't notice I was sweating already. Right then he got up and turned toward me. When he saw me moving away from him, he stopped and said, "Are you serious?"

What was I supposed to say to that? What about this was so confusing for him? I started to really sweat then. Did he truly not understand, or did he think what I'd suggested was inappropriate? I missed tech support right then.

"Yes, look, you find yourself another match. I know it can be a hassle, but I'm sure it won't be too bad, I mean, you're a young, attractive man."

Roger was looking at me intently, and I still couldn't figure out what that look was supposed to communicate, if it was questioning or defiant. There was no way to be sure, so I opted for questioning, the most logical. "The data says finding a match is easiest for a man in your condition."

Roger looked at me. Surprised? I felt I had to defuse the situation, which was supposed to be a simple conversation between colleagues.

"Our work is starting to suffer, and I think it's because our neurotransmitter levels have dipped. I don't know how to fix mine, I'll figure that out next, but there's an easy enough solution for you. Which is another match, to get the levels back up."

Roger's eyes stared into mine, and I got the impression that something inside their infinite blue had been snuffed out. But then they suddenly filled up with light, and he said, "OK."

It made me really happy to see his light eyes shining again, and I went back to my desk.

When Roger found a substitute, it should have cheered me up, but instead, visions of him with his new match got mixed up with the worms in my head, their slime stroking my skin, my nasal passages. It was my own fault, of course, because I was the one who asked him to show me her profile. She was a blonde they found on Datayou. She had very light eyes, like Roger's.

I couldn't get the visions of them kissing out of my head. I saw Roger running his hands along her inner thighs (that was something I really liked), saw her caressing his hair (one of the things he really liked), then it all got jumbled up with the slime from the worms inching their way from my feet to my knees, covering me in that sticky, disgusting slime, which, against all odds, felt good.

Instead of disappearing, my problems multiplied. On one side, there was that feeling of sinking, as if the worms were dragging me down to their slimy underworld; on the other, the visions of Roger and the blonde; and to top it all off, we weren't making any progress. Our decline in productivity—the graph charting our progress took its biggest nosedive yet—the slime, and the visions of the blonde were starting to get to me.

One of my problems, however, was quickly solved. Manuela put the blonde at Roger's old desk. She sent a message to the three of us: "It's about time we filled this spot, three minds are always better than two. Have fun!"

So, I didn't have to imagine her anymore. She was right there.

She was more attractive in person than in her profile. Her skin was radiant, not only because she hadn't hit thirty yet, but also because the intercourse with Roger was working. Every time I looked up and saw her, I was reminded I'd gone six weeks without sex, and everything I was experiencing was most likely because my cerebrum was wasting away, starved for endorphins and dopamine.

Roger seemed cheerful. He'd gone back to making jokes about how drugs make the world go round, suggesting we incorporate them in our statistical framework. The blonde laughed—a pure laugh, crystalline, like her eyes and Roger's—but I was incapable, my brain was treading water.

Scenes of the two of them tore into me the moment I closed my eyes and tried to sleep. I imagined them in her bed—Roger didn't like to have sex at his place, he said it wasn't tidy enough. The bed frame was white, a Gaspard with drawers underneath that made it look like an antique dresser, because the blonde had good taste but was also junior, so she could only afford to buy furniture at IKEA, their pricier items, but still, IKEA. I thought about that furniture and almost missed my time as a junior employee, at my first company, barely making rent but feeling the glee of just starting out. I saw the blonde on top (Roger's favorite position), his eyes rolling back (which happened automatically when he liked something), one of his hands on the slatted IKEA headboard (she chose it because it was practical and made the room feel cohesive and calm), the other grabbing her ass (because that's what turned him on most). Then she let out a moan, and that turned him on even more, and the two of them fused in a flood of dopamine, endorphins, and oxytocin that would keep them in peak form all week.

Roger and the blonde started generating results, but I was still in a dry spell. They had managed to fashion an algorithm that sorted through all our new data. Our productivity went up, not all the way back to our optimal level, but the worst of it was over, we were beginning to catch up with the other six teams.

Manuela sent a message to the three of us. "Well done, you. Whatever you're doing, it's working. You've really turned things around. Can you imagine the number of problems we'll solve? Next stop, happiness."

Roger and the blonde arrived at some interesting findings: what made people happiest, it seemed, wasn't lots of money or lots of things or being able to buy something regardless of the price, but rather the acquisition of experiences. The possibility of reliving them and describing them was what led to true satisfaction.

Nevertheless, according to the data, it was much harder to acquire an experience than an object. Going on vacation, for example, an action among those that yield the highest levels of happiness, is complex. For it to be satisfactory, other components must be taken into account. Time, organizational skills, the presence of a companion—traveling alone is beneficial, evidently, but less so than traveling with someone. Changes in these variables could reduce the effectiveness of the experience in the long run, so at least the following had to be accounted for in the algorithm: the possibility that a subject would lack an adequate companion, the possibility that the companion would appear adequate but later prove not to be, the possibility that something would go wrong on the trip—here, the variables, from falling ill unexpectedly, to dissatisfaction with accommodations or transport, were so plentiful it was tough to capture them all—and apart from all that was the destination itself, which could also be unsatisfactory for some reason. The range of potential outcomes seemed almost infinite.

If we wanted to do real science, we had to include all that in our analysis, didn't we? I had always wanted to do work that mattered, but even more than that, to do science, so I wrote up a list of every possible variable we needed to account for in evaluating the relationship between happiness and acquiring experiences, and I sent it to Manuela and copied the rest of WhiteAngel.

The moment they opened it, Roger and the blonde came over to my desk. They had moved me so I was next to the window. The city, viewed from above, looked like a huge organism, the street that led to our building was its spinal column, the trees in nearby parks doubled as fur, it moved like it was stretching, waking up. The parallel avenues, where cars jolted along and people came and went, endlessly attending to the details of their lives, were its arms and its legs. From our window you couldn't distinguish their clothing, just a multicolor smudge of coats combatting the winter chill, but they probably all wore perfume, and had shiny hair, and were hoping for ten-of-ten days, on which they would finally solve all their problems. I liked thinking about how, up here, we were working on it for them, trying to make all their dreams come true.

"You've gone too far," Roger said.

At first I thought he was kidding, that it was another one of his jokes. The day before, he'd joked that we should incorporate porn in our calculations. The blonde had laughed in a way that gave me pause. What if she wasn't so pure after all? Maybe she liked it rough, and those light eyes, that near-imperceptible makeup, were hiding a nympho-maniac.

It could happen, stranger things have. In fact, statistics we weren't to factor in, since it went against the company's code of ethics, suggested that what really made fifteen percent of the population happy were certain sexual aberrations.

But it was obviously unreasonable to take that information into account, because what if the thing that made someone happy was zoophilia? Would we then promote the behavior? No, there were lines we wouldn't cross. "Society has to be pleased, but also polite," and that's our responsibility too. It was in the welcome speech, I remember perfectly. And we had it hanging over our desk, although there was no real need, since that data wasn't supposed to reach us. But somehow Roger managed to get his hands on it. Often, when he was drinking, he'd boast that he knew the deep web like the back of his hand, including who knows how many dark secrets he'd never reveal.

It wasn't that far-fetched to think the angelic blonde might have been addicted to S&M, or a necrophile, or something else entirely. It was even possible Roger liked that. Why not? I'd never asked. I had assumed our standard sexual encounters satisfied him.

"You've gone too far," Roger repeated.

That's when I knew without a doubt he was angry, he wouldn't have said the phrase twice if he weren't.

"Why?"

"What do you mean *why*? You want me to explain?"

The blonde seemed indignant too, though with features that delicate—thin eyebrows (maybe plucked), tiny nose, insubstantial lips, round and diminutive chin—it was hard to say.

I weighed responses and chose the most neutral one, which I delivered in as calm a tone as possible. "I would like it if you'd explain, if you don't mind."

Roger shot me a look of, I think, rage, though it could also have been a sudden sharp pain in some region of his body. But he had never mentioned chronic pain before, so it must have been rage.

"What am I supposed to explain? What is there to explain. What were you trying to do when you sent your report to Manuela? You want them to fire all three of us?"

I wasn't sure what to say. Roger had always been better at reading people's intentions than me, that's why I found the thought of explaining mine to him absurd, but since I could see that he was waiting for me to respond, I said, "No, of course not, why would I want them to fire us? You know this job is my life."

"Then what were you trying to do?"

In truth, I hadn't asked myself that question. Had I been trying to do something? I couldn't figure out what Roger wanted to hear. I reviewed the sequence of events: I'd gone over the algorithm, checked its functionality, thought about possible errors, about my directives.

"I was trying to improve our work," I said. "Checking for weak spots, suggesting solutions. Same as always."

"Same as always?"

Roger shook his head. I couldn't tell if he meant that it wasn't the same as always, or that he didn't like my improvements.

There was a ding from our inboxes. It was Manuela, she had written to the three of us:

"Dear team WhiteAngel: your results are being reanalyzed and we'll keep your suggestions in mind, but remember, science takes time. We can't do it all at once, can we? One step at a time, now. We'll get there."

I thought the message seemed encouraging, nice, like her messages usually were. But Roger disagreed. "Now do you see what you've done?" he yelled, and shot me his fatal look, the one he reserved for unfriendly servers and pizza delivery guys. "This is a goddamn disaster."

Blasco

Ever since I found Laila, I long for the clock to strike seven so I can log on.

Before, I contented myself with visiting xxx.com every so often, opening a window at random, almost indifferent to what appeared on the other side. I would look at breasts, suggestions of them underneath cotton t-shirts, the somewhat infantile curve of a navel above jean shorts, and that was stimulation enough for me.

The image quality wasn't high. They looked like videos someone had taken using an outdated cellphone. But that provided a touch of realism that made the whole experience very effective.

The girls were normally lying in bed, watching TV or flipping through magazines, sometimes combing their hair, looking in the mirror. Occasionally, they put lipstick on. Then they undid one shirt button, or slid a strap off one shoulder, and like that, the window would close.

To see more, you had to pay extra. But I simply went back to the homepage, opened another window, and watched the next one.

It was a hobby like any other, I told myself. Some people go to fancy restaurants, pay for massages or experimental concerts, and I spent my time peering into bedrooms where there was always some pink detail, a teddy bear or a bedspread, and almost always, on the walls, posters of North American cities: San Francisco, Seattle, New York.

I saw myself as a detective looking for clues. Who were these girls? They seemed like average pampered daughters of middle-class families. Their bedrooms were what you'd find in any single-family home in the suburbs, with fitted wardrobes, built-in shelving, and windows through which I discerned the branches of trees. Although those windows were always covered by blinds or lace curtains, so the image I thought I was glimpsing may well have been an illusion or a projection.

Sometimes they would look directly at the camera. That, for me, was the shining moment. Their eyes had the irrepressible gleam you only see in the eyes of those who have yet to renounce anything, when stupidity is still indistinguishable from innocence, and that drove me absolutely wild.

When Laila appeared, I'd been ensnared for weeks already, trying to escape the lethal monotony of my life.

I spent my time evaluating investments for long-standing clients while Diana, my wife, kept the entire enterprise in the black. In the course of a typical day, we barely crossed paths. At six, we went down to the parking garage for the car.

Driving was the only male privilege I retained. It made Diana nervous, she liked to avoid it. Therefore, for twenty minutes a day, we could pass for what I see as a typical couple: a husband driving home his loving wife.

When we arrived home, we showered in our own bathrooms and

put on comfortable clothes. I stayed in the study with my computer, she went to the living room and paged through travel magazines. Sometimes we cooked dinner, but usually we heated up something premade or ordered a pizza.

They say living together ruins a couple, but that seems a bit trite to me. To my mind, our situation had one cause alone. If Latoya hadn't gotten cancer, we would never have careened into this swamp.

Latoya said she was grateful for her illness. And she wasn't being ironic in the least, nor was she trying to make us feel good, to alleviate our guilt because it had gotten her and no one else. She really meant it, hand on her heart, humbly lowering her long eyelids.

On weekends, when she arrived at whatever restaurant our friend group had chosen, the anticipation was palpable. The proximity to death made everyone crazy. No one tired of hearing about the side effects of her treatment, the revelations she'd had, how she now cherished even the minor details of her life: the taste of her morning coffee, the breeze on the back of her neck since she'd lost her hair.

Everyone showered her with attention. Can you eat that? Would you rather we head out now? Is the noise too much for you? One possible side effect of chemotherapy, it seems, is being bothered by, nay, unable to tolerate, things you've never thought twice about before.

Yes, no, no, she said, beaming. Before she got sick, she rarely smiled. I wondered if her treatment didn't also include some opiate, one good old Latoya wasn't aware of. Up until a few months ago, no one had paid much attention to her, because everyone was fixated on my wife.

Diana had engineered things so she was always the most stylish one in the group, the only woman in a real management position, higher up in the company's hierarchy than her own husband. And that husband—me—simply adored her.

She was the perfect totem. The women in the group envied her and therefore criticized her constantly, though never to her face, and in the men, she awakened the fiercest desire, the desire to be dominated.

All that envy nourished our marital bed and kept us, if not happy, at least in acceptable spirits. It was our golden age.

When attention on Latoya began to wane, I held fast to the hope things would go back to normal, but that's when Efe made her big announcement.

We met for dinner at a pulperia, which we rarely did, since there were usually more appetizing options: more fashionable, vegan, Thai, raw, or deconstructed.

Efe took the floor. She'd had too much to drink. It's not that the rest of us didn't drink, but all of us observed a certain limit. We were exemplary in that way.

The group was slow to react, immersed in the usual conversations. Latoya was describing one of her therapy epiphanies. She always used that word, as if chemo and radiation were just like visits to a psychologist, simple and perfectly painless. Carlos was talking about the fluctuation in wheat prices in Ethiopia, business prospects, or his favorite trendy new bar.

Carlos didn't often come to our gatherings. Though the rule remained unspoken, these were gatherings for couples, and as far as we were aware, he'd been unable to keep a relationship going past the one-week mark. He was a small anomaly in our compact group, fulfilling a dual purpose: we felt good about ourselves for welcoming him in, and he reminded us all how lucky we were.

What no one could understand is why he cared to join us from time to time instead of going out in search of prey. But he always seemed to enjoy himself, or maybe he just came to appease Diana. That's how it was with her cubs; with them, she had absolute power. They looked up at her, eyes shining, each sure he was the chosen one, the one who would become her right-hand man. Nobody ever realized that Diana had no intention of singling anyone out, she was perfectly content with her traveling court, and raising the rank of another would have meant risking her own position. But they were incapable of accepting that, because when they interviewed for assistant jobs, they were always promised promotions, and that was enough to keep their hopes alive.

It was Latoya, I think, who asked, "What do you mean you're leaving?"

"We have to," Efe said. "It's relocate or get laid off."

The avalanche was immediate: When, where, for how long? What about the kids?

Each response provoked greater agitation. Indefinitely, we don't know if we'll be back, the kids will have to adjust, we're not the first people this has happened to.

I detected no bitterness in Efe's voice. In fact, she was talking as if they had won the lottery. They were game, and everyone sensed it. For weeks, the topic of employee "relocation" had been in the air. The adventure of an unexpected move to a new country—normally somewhere in the Persian Gulf, though we'd also heard of others, in rare instances, sent to countries in Europe, or to the U.S.—the exotic appeal, the linguistic challenges that would pay off in the end, what's better than multilingualism, especially for the kids.

Diana had been thinking we should travel somewhere new over the holidays, and she quickly scrapped the idea. It was an escape plan that had, very briefly, roused a certain excitement. But now nothing was more worthy of admiration than relocating, and she knew it.

Because we had determined that the "relocated" would acquire a new identity, nothing less: a new "I." Who doesn't want a new "I"? It was the highest form of adventure.

Diana tried to jump on the bandwagon. At every opportunity, she remarked on how brave the two of them were. But her comments fell on deaf ears.

The phrases Diana had used every time she brought up the idea of the trip, like "change up our routine," or "have a real experience," started to sound old-fashioned, and from that moment on, she lost interest.

When the travel magazines disappeared from our home, my wife and I were confronted with the most desolate void of our lives.

She went to the doctor for migraines that started assailing her at night. They prescribed some pills she took two at a time, convinced they would help with the pain. I was never sure if she just preferred that version of events, or if the doctor had failed to explain that her migraines were no more than a symptom of anxiety, which he was surely tired of diagnosing, and, to make matters worse, had no idea how to treat.

The pills kept her on her feet, but outside of our marathon workdays, for which she seemed to have been programmed, no trace of my wife's enthusiasm remained. It was difficult to believe that the person who, by day, directed the entire investment division of a huge company, made everyone dance to her tune, was incapable of lifting a finger at home. Her movements were restricted to donning pajamas and watching TV.

That's how we were, two bodies cast into existence to orbit each other without ever touching, when Laila appeared.

Laila was an explosion. She was wearing a shirt that went down to her knees, with writing across the chest: "College Girl."

She's no more attractive than the others; in fact, her nose might be a little long, and her lips are extremely thin, but everything about her is hypnotic.

Normally she's sitting in bed, leaned back against a couple of pillows, reading. She doesn't lift up her shirt, doesn't show you her belly button, doesn't lie back to reveal her breasts.

The day I found her, she was reading *Moby Dick*, then she moved on to *The Fall of the House of Usher*. Now, she's reading *Twilight*.

She reads it all with equal voracity, you can almost guess from her expression which scenes are running through her mind: the heroic and also ridiculous search for the sea monster, Poe's darkness, sexual tension between teenagers.

I'm intrigued by her versatility and her taste for being watched. In her expression, there's the audacity of someone who thinks she has everything under control. She's the ultimate prize, and she knows it. I guess that's why she came up under "recommended for you."

In the two weeks since I first saw her, I've contented myself with watching what happens up until the moment her window closes. But I'm dying to know what it'd be like if I stayed a little longer, paid a little more to go on.

With the others, I felt no curiosity at all, they would take off their shirts and stay in their bras. They would expose their small, firm breasts without thinking, because their bras were made of transparent fabric, like flies' wings. Then they would disconnect. After the third charge, they'd take off their pants or their skirt and leave their thighs bare, maybe they'd turn around, but not all the way, just partly, so you could see the side of the buttocks. That would satisfy some, they'd come before the fourth disconnection. But others would want more and would keep going, and then they'd take off their bras and let you see their breasts for an instant before lying face down, using their own bodies to cover up. For some, their partial nakedness was sufficient. But a few days later, those who once stopped at the first disconnection would be paying for part two, those who had been content with part two would be going on to part three, and it would proceed that way until they got to the last one, in which the women revealed their full bodies, not for long, just enough to inspire dreams about caressing every inch, burying your mouth in every corner. After a while, that wouldn't be enough, either, and then they would pay for the next level. First the girls would run their hands over their breasts, naked, then they would stroke their stomachs, and later on, their bodies entirely visible, they would touch themselves. And before long, that wouldn't be enough either.

But what would Laila do?

The question consumes me, especially since today has been so difficult. In October, for no apparent reason, it appears that investor confidence has gone down. The client I've been advising has refused to move on anything, and as he delivered the bad news, he laughed with a spontaneity I myself have lacked for some time, since I don't dare do anything that could so much as raise an eyebrow. He, on the other hand, showed up in comfortable, worn-out jeans, while I'd just managed to bring myself to knot the green company tie, which I find more and more oppressive, because despite the chill that has taken hold of the city, the air from the vents in the office comes out burning hot and smothers us.

Laila is wearing a sleeveless top, gray and a little faded, and some jean shorts that show off her thighs. As usual, she begins reading, lying back against the pillows. You get the sense she's completely worry-free.

Her eyes are the only things that move, from one side to the other, traversing the lines of *The Stranger*. With each movement, I can feel her going deeper into the North African summer heat, journeying, with Meursault, to the home where his mother's body lies, the temperature at the burial nearly suffocates her, and the following morning, she sets off for the beach. At that point, surely once Meursault has already gone in for a swim, she disconnects.

Almost without thinking, I click the button to keep watching, and the moment I do, I start to shake. I feel I'm plunging into emptiness and think I'd be better off if I closed the computer, but I don't.

Laila reappears on the screen. Her appearance is unchanged.

I'm outraged. Is that what I paid for? To watch the same thing again? I wait. She keeps reading. Surely Meursault is already with Marie Cardona, maybe fondling her breasts, maybe swimming with her, grabbing her by the waist. Suddenly something changes, her breathing speeds up, she sighs or moans.

I hold my breath and wait to see what happens, and right then, without warning, the window closes.

Angélica

No one talks about Hester anymore.

When I started at the Plant three years ago, people would say things. The medical technologists said Hester was meticulous when it came to requesting lab work. The receptionist sometimes reminded me that she always finished patient visits on time. All that eagerness to communicate that my predecessor was, in every way, superior would have put some people on edge. But the things they said didn't bother me, they sounded like an echo, the echo of a life struggling to affirm itself, to belong, struggling against death.

Several weeks after I started in her role, another fertility specialist, Fabio, mistook me for her. I was headed back from the bathroom when I felt a hand on my shoulder, and someone said, "Hester?"

As soon as I turned around, he looked down, embarrassed, and stuttered, "Ah, sorry, Angélica," then walked in the other direction as fast as he could. Later, he explained that Hester and I had similar builds; apart from our hair—mine a little darker, shorter—we looked exactly the same from behind.

That detail only heightened my interest. I tried to figure out what had become of Hester, but when I asked my colleagues on coffee breaks or over occasional beers, they shrugged or said no one knew anything.

I couldn't understand why, if she had really been so beloved, no one was keeping in touch with her.

I searched for her, in vain, on social media. All the Hester Garcías I found were teenagers posting selfies. There was no trace of her on the internet, either—as if she had never existed. I had begun to accept the fact that Hester was one more unsolved mystery, lumped her in with the mass of unanswered questions that now seemed to make up my life, when I came across her notebook.

I was reorganizing my office to make room for Lisa when I found it. Management had said they would finally bring in help for me—after innumerable emails explaining that I was drowning, that my work was going to suffer if things went on as they were—but the two of us would have to make do with one office. They brought in an extra table, chair, and computer, so Lisa could do consultations and answer emails I didn't have time for.

In order to fit the new table, I had to move my desk and push the filing cabinets behind the door, which meant you couldn't open it fully. The chairs where patients sat were now a little too close together.

We had to get rid of some furniture, so I got two big trash bags and started to empty the cabinets. The clinic was closed for the day, and you could hear the cleaners dragging their carts up and down the halls. Occasionally their laughter would fill the air. During work hours, no one laughed, we smiled at most, and talked in hushed tones, sometimes holding back tears when things went wrong. So that laughter sounded strange, like hearing the roar of an unknown animal when you're camping and trying to sleep.

In the upper drawers, there were outdated pamphlets the Plant used to give patients on their first visits. I tossed them in one of the bags without thinking too much and kept going. In the middle ones were old planners with the company logo on the front—it was supposed to look like the silhouette of a pregnant person, but it made me think of the boa constrictor that swallows its prey whole in *The Little Prince*— and also office supplies, yellowing sheets of paper, and some colored markers and dried-up correction fluid. I threw it all out.

In the bottom drawer was a mess of notebooks emblazoned with the old company motto: The Plant, where happiness is made. They must have been for promotional purposes, but they looked outdated now: the covers, green or red, were too bright, and the type—casual, juvenile—didn't help. I felt a little guilty getting rid of them, but anyway, nobody uses paper now, so I didn't know who we would give them to. I put them in the second bag and went to call over the cleaners.

But then I saw something in one of the open notebooks. There were lines of numbers and letters:

"I—34—EF—5A—2M—F."

I picked it up, slid it into my bag, and let them know they could clear out the office.

Before I got in bed, I looked through the notebook. Page after page had been filled with lines of random letters and numbers, which didn't look good for Hester—it seemed likely she'd been dealing with some kind of mental illness. Maybe something like OCD or schizophrenia. I'd seen patients do similar things when I was a psychiatric resident. That would explain her extreme meticulousness, which seemed bordering on obsessive. If she'd experienced an episode, she may have been sent to a clinic or whisked off to some relative's home. That would also explain why there was no trace of her online, maybe her family shut down her accounts, or maybe she'd started to go by another name, cut ties with her medical history.

I left Hester's notebook on my nightstand, next to *On the Origin of Species* and the antiaging cream I never used. I had resolved to read Darwin at night before falling asleep, having left it unfinished since college. I was haunted by the voice of my molecular genetics professor: "You'll know nothing of evolution until you've read this book." For years I'd ignored his advice, but then I got it into my head that maybe Darwin could help me right the capsizing ship of my life.

The problem was, I arrived home so exhausted I couldn't make it past the introduction. Normally I would get stuck in the spot where Darwin says, "My work is now (1859) nearly finished; but as it will take me two or three more years to complete it, and as my health is far from strong, I have been urged to publish this Abstract." At that point, I would stop and ask myself what kind of person thought a text almost five hundred pages long qualified as an abstract, and right then I'd fall asleep, usually with the open book on my chest.

Like *On the Origin of Species*, Hester's notebook collected dust on my nightstand, until everything that was happening led me back to it.

A while after Lisa showed up, I started to feel like things at work weren't going the way I'd hoped they would. At first I didn't think much of it, because almost all of what I experienced struck me as strange back then, as if the order of things were jumbled and there were only random events that, even taken together, completely lacked meaning. So the fact that we had fewer and fewer successful pregnancies didn't seem outside the bounds of possibility. Plus it was mostly a hunch I had, based on the cases I supervised personally. I couldn't access all the Plant's official data.

Not even fertility specialists could make use of the general records, only open cases, and only at the time of consultation. Afterward, access to even those records was restricted. It was because of healthcare data privacy, or that's what they told us during our training.

But two weeks before the annual meeting I couldn't stop thinking about it, so I shared my impressions with Lisa. She only said that there was no basis for my theory and that I was probably just exhausted. Then she smiled like a mom does when her child makes a small error and pulled her hair into a ponytail. She showed up every day with perfect curls and flawless makeup. I envied that, in a way: her dark, shiny curls, composed of symmetrical curves, implied she had mastered a universal order I would never have access to.

It was a struggle for me to look presentable every morning. When I got out of bed, I appeared to have just returned from a hike in the jungle, my hair, neither curly nor straight, ballooned into huge knots, and most days, I opted to wash it again to regain some semblance of control. Even then, I could never achieve the look I was after. Every facet of my being seemed to rebel against the order that others navigated with ease.

The closer we got to the annual meeting, the more unnerved I felt. Lisa's response had failed to soothe me. If our success rate were even hinted at publicly, it was going to be a problem. The regional director couldn't ignore something like that.

The prospect of being fired brought me back to the world of the living. With no family to turn to, and no partner to rely on, unemployment looked to me like falling completely into the void. I reviewed our protocols over and over, trying to figure out where we were going wrong, but there was nothing.

I started to have trouble sleeping, and during one bout of insomnia, the week of the annual meeting, it dawned on me that Hester's notebook was a record of case outcomes:

"1—34 years—External Fertilization—5 Attempts—2 Miscarriages—Failure."

In total, Hester had notated 1,140 cases. Of those, 80 percent had been unsuccessful. The failure rate was ascending. Over 73 percent, if you looked at the first hundred cases. Almost 90 if you looked at just the last hundred. It was abysmal, especially compared to the story we told the public.

I started notating cases in Hester's notebook. I added twelve before the annual meeting. The success rate continued to plummet.

The Plant rented a conference hall downtown, close to the restaurant where we were going for dinner. I put on a black velvet dress and indestructible sheer tights that made my legs look longer. At another point in my life, when I took my appearance much more seriously, I maintained an arsenal of accessories and styles for all occasions, and from time to time, I still used them out of habit. If I'd had to go out and buy something, I might have skipped the meeting altogether, under the pretext of being sick. The mere idea of approaching a clothing store made me anxious. I smoothed my hair and put it in a tight, low ponytail, a last resort, but I had no time for anything else. A trip to the salon, which always smelled newly remodeled, was filled with the chatter of stylists, and demanded devotion to haircare products, was totally out of the question.

My colleagues strictly observed the rules of propriety: the women wore dark satin suits, the men wore tailored pants and jackets. Festive but restrained, appropriate for the scientific community in late September.

I sat down next to Lisa, who looked almost the same as she did every day, except for her hair, which, instead of being gently pulled back at the nape of her neck, was completely loose, somehow without subtracting an iota of her polish. She was wearing a slightly higher heel than usual. I felt bad for her, she had no idea what was coming.

The ambient light went down, and out came the regional director, in a shawl and a floral-print dress that seemed a little extravagant, more appropriate for a wedding. She started her speech with the requisite phrase, "Our purpose here is to save lives, we have the best job in the world." We applauded, an applause that was gentle, but approving. Right then they turned on the screen behind her, where they would usually project data, the company's future plans, and any key takeaways. I swallowed.

But to my surprise, the flood never came. The regional director was "thrilled with our dedication and skill, the numbers speak for themselves," patient volume was up by so much they'd be opening two new clinics, "there's so much for us to celebrate tonight."

She concluded her speech in the same way as always: "You are the crew of Apollo 11. You are the bearers of hope. Enjoy the party."

The bathroom at the restaurant was bigger than my house. Covered in black marble, it looked like a mausoleum. The walls, the sinks, the floor, everything gleamed under halogen lights, with that subtle matte shine polished stone surfaces have. Only the faucets, towel dispensers, and mirror frames, which were gold, suspended the hypnotic effect of the marble.

Despite the floral air freshener and the fabric-softener scent wafting from two small pyramids of towels stacked next to the sinks, I could detect the faint, sour odor of vomit. It was clear I wasn't the only one who overdid it with the gin. I touched up my lipstick and dabbed my neck with a damp towel. Hester's notes went around and around in my head.

I could have used Lisa's help just then, but she'd left before dessert. She was always slipping off early. She didn't like parties, and more than that, she didn't like to be around drunk people. "I'm just not on that wavelength," she sometimes said.

I looked in the mirror, smiled, and told myself several times I had made the whole thing up, I was simply overthinking, a side effect of exhaustion, it plays tricks on you, that's all. You start to distort things, or you see problems where there are none.

I tried to focus on Lisa, she was always so serene, like a light I could grab on to. I thought about how lucky I was to work alongside her, and then I took a breath and went out to the dance floor, ready to take a step forward in life, out of that thicket of doubt and suspicion.

The room had filled with men in extravagant suits. Nothing like ours. They were trying to move, but their bodies didn't respond, it was like their dancing function had been disabled. Some of them went over to the women who hovered nearby. They were so gorgeous you wanted to touch them, just to confirm they were real and not hallucinations. The enchantresses, probably hired to make the atmosphere feel more festive, had facial expressions of boredom and vague distress.

Others approached my colleagues, who also mostly ignored them. The men in extravagant suits were striking out.

One of them came over to me, he wasn't wearing a jacket and had rolled up the sleeves of his shirt, and the chest was stained, maybe he'd spilled some wine. His eyes were wild from alcohol and cocaine.

"Something's up with those girls, don't you think?" he said.

"What?" I replied.

"Yeah, they're a little crazy. They have that thing, I don't know, like they're saviors or something. They say some weird shit. I'm Carlos, by the way."

And it suddenly occurred to me that his destructive and innocent language was the first real thing I'd heard in months.

It's been weeks since the annual party, and to my surprise, I have yet to receive the dreaded call from the regional director. I was sure Lisa and I would be summoned, that they'd ask for explanations, that everything they said that night was a cover-up, but no. Nothing has happened.

I try to forget about the data and Hester's notebook, try to convince myself we're both wrong. Isn't it possible that my perceptions are incomplete for some reason I can't identify, and the same thing happened to Hester? It's not my most scientific hypothesis, but I'm going to have to run with it. I'm done with this vital drift. It's leading me nowhere.

I concentrate on Carlos, who lives completely outside of my worries and never stops making plans. Tonight he's invited me out to a sushi place he saw in the Sunday supplement.

When the food arrives, Carlos bows to it.

"It's the best in the city," he says. He wrinkles his nose and takes a bite.

Really, he doesn't like sushi, and neither do I. Not the dehydrated seaweed, not the gohan.

"Smells like piss," Carlos whispers when they bring out the miso soup.

And the whole scenario, that we think the food tastes terrible, that the waiters are young and handsome, that the prices are exorbitant, that the rest of the diners talk in hushed tones and make gestures of slight indignation but never smile—no one does in fashionable restaurants—all that makes us feel like we're in heaven.

The evening ends in my bed, when Carlos comes in his condom with an irrepressible moan and then wraps me in his arms.

"You're so special," he says while he strokes my hair.

And his words, surely well intentioned, sound hollow.

I should say something similar back, tell him yes, he's special too, let myself be pulled along by the current of his warm body and his embrace. I run my fingers through his honey-colored hair, which he always gels so it's shiny. But no words come out. I get up and throw the condom away. That semen is certainly special, the product of Carlos's soft, supple body, not like what we have to use at the lab, which comes mostly from imperfect donors, older husbands.

With material like this, we'd get results for sure, I think. And my anxiety comes back and consumes it all: Carlos and his love, what he calls love, Carlos and my chance to lead a life according to basic principles that seem to work for everyone else in the world.

Though I try my absolute best to avoid it, I end up looking at Hester's notebook again, and noting down new cases. Still, I'm trying not to take it too seriously. I'm concentrating on Carlos and his quick wit, his crackling ideas.

We're taking the metro to Rey and Fabio's party. Carlos loves parties, and now that we've been together two months, I've run out of excuses not to go with him. We wanted to call an Uber, but it was impossible, the taxis are striking again. I don't know why they bother, everyone knows they're going to disappear.

Our car is packed. The second we step in, we're hit with an odor, a mixture of gasoline, sweat, and fast food that makes you nauseous. Observing the other passengers is inevitable. One family in particular catches my eye.

There must be twenty or so of them, three generations: the grandfather and grandmother, their children, sons- and daughters-in-law, and maybe ten grandkids of various ages. Impossible to say who is the child of whom. Their clothing is unusual: the men are in dress coats and suits, maroon or black satin, the women are stuffed into shiny dresses, mauve for the older ones, orange for the girls, and they have on pleather jackets. The littlest girls wear white cotton dresses. You can tell they're all uncomfortable, the men keep adjusting their pants, the women, checking their necklines. When they move that way, they resemble a kind of plant, a giant flower that shakes in the wind running through the car, their dresses snapping sweetly like petals in the breeze, the men's heavy sighs like stems creaking under the weight of leaves and seeds.

The women murmur stories, how the grandfather tried to run off when the grandmother got pregnant, how the great-grandfather went to the train station to find him, how they forced him to come back... They laugh venomously. The mothers wipe snot from kids' noses and lament the passage of time. The grandfather, who has been standing for fifteen stops, makes a gesture, and a daughter or daughter-in-law gets up and gives him her seat. He turns to sit down, and seeing his face, I realize he's blind in one eye. Still, he seems content. That one eye radiates tranquility, and as he observes his brood, his mouth takes on a satisfied expression.

I can't stop looking. Who are they? How did they get their gametes to function so well with no intervention? Is there a special formula, something they've been keeping secret from the rest of the population?

Then Carlos, who notices my fascination, whispers in my ear: "Must be a Roma wedding. Think they got enough hair oil?" And for a moment that seems to explain everything, the joy that emanates from their movements, their very high birthrate, the Plant's declining numbers.

I let myself be lulled by Carlos's ease with snap judgments. I try to think like him, feel what he feels. That lightness. That lack of curiosity people call self-esteem.

We make a pretty retinue. Muted but priceless outfits; invisible, mattifying makeup; smiles ready to overcome anything. My co-workers from the Plant keep saying things like: "Love between men is so beautiful," and "taking that step," and "sharing your life with another person," "that's generosity worth celebrating." Rey and Fabio smile so much it seems like their faces might break. The baby is quiet in his crib for most of the evening. I don't know where they got him, but he looks like a baby from an ad.

The hosts bring out trays of little pearls that look like caviar but aren't, they're aromatized, texturized soy, so as not to offend our arteries or our fragile sensibilities. There are other unrecognizable items, gelatinous, made of superfoods, chia seeds, quinoa-flour puff pastry. On the terrace, where the party ends up after midnight, they've put out heaters to protect us from the sudden November cold, and garlands of lights, white but diffuse, that make the space feel magical, perfect for confessions.

This is how we construct paradise.

Carlos comes from behind and encircles me in his arms, right as I'm taking a bite of the caviar that's not caviar, which has an unpleasant aftertaste I can't pinpoint—acidity, bitterness? He takes my hand and leads me to the edge of the terrace, and when I'm about to tell him I'm terrified of heights, he whispers, "What do you think, babe? Should we give it a try?"

María

Because of the worms, because Roger and I were a perfect match, but he and the blonde were more perfect, but most of all because of the scientific method, I've ended up in a therapist's office.

The chairs in the office are immaculate white. I don't remember them being like that. Of course, the last time I was here, it was February, like now, except I had just come back from Seattle, and compared to the Emerald City, here, everything is gray. If they had asked, I would have said I remembered the furniture in a more neutral shade, one that was harder to name.

In Seattle, the walls of buildings shone, the signs on them shone, even though they were made entirely of recycled, ecologically friendly materials. People's faces shone, everything did, even in midwinter.

I loved Felicia, our facilitator, from day one. She wore no makeup and unfashionable glasses, and her lively eyes left me breathless. We all listened to her, open-mouthed:

"Now, I'd like you to break into groups and imagine that a start-up obliterates all your firm's business."

We broke into groups. It was like we were scrambling to do what the president ordered, what's she saying now, we obeyed the same way we would have if she were the king of the universe. At that point, our company wasn't doing big data yet, only statistics. We were living in prehistory.

It only took us half a day to dismantle our businesses and rebuild. The team was undeniably brilliant. There was Marize, a woman from Brazil who'd attained the highest standing in calculus in the country; Takito, a man from Japan who had designed a system for forecasting tsunamis twenty times more effective than previous methods; and Adèle, who we'd suspected was only there because she was attractive and sleeping with her French boss, until the moment came to present creative solutions and we got to watch her "do her thing," which was basically entering into a trance. She closed her eyes and made a high-pitched noise, almost a whine, and suddenly, she opened them and described an outrageous idea that never would have occurred to you. And it worked.

We presented our summary to Felicia, and she gave us a look of approval. "I knew you were capable, that's why I chose you," she said, and she winked.

That wink sealed the deal, we had to fight the urge to throw ourselves at her feet, to swear eternal fealty. We managed to contain it, of course. Our companies had spent too much on airfare for us to get on her nerves right away. Also, the fee for the course was two thirds of my annual salary.

What was in Seattle? We walked along the city streets—the facilitators explained that in the U.S., no one walks, but they do, because it's natural, and they weren't willing to live in a city where you need a car to get around—and I don't know if it was the smell of organic bakeries, the municipal lighting (energy efficient), or the laughter of people leaving their offices (light, easy), but it was like walking through paradise, or even better, since paradise must be odorless, beautiful but untouchable, and in Seattle, everything gave off a scent that was wild but comforting at the same time. Marize said how good it smelled, and Felicia was quick to respond:

"We have two mountain ranges less than an hour away, the Cascades and the Olympics, and the ocean, too, we could never work in a city too far from the mountains and the ocean, it's just not good for you."

At that point we still didn't know who Felicia meant when she said "we," it could have been her family, or Felicia and her partner. It wasn't long before we learned that "we" was her research team. It was the company creatives, the founders, who were unwilling to live in a city that was disconnected from nature.

That conversation with Felicia is what sent me to the therapist's office the first time. I felt horrible when I got back from the trip, missing something I'd never had but that I now yearned for with every breath. Yes, the trip to Seattle paid off in the medium-term, mostly because it led to my joining Manuela and WhiteAngel, but it also destabilized me and made the chairs in the therapist's office seem grayer than they were. I guess if I can see how bright they are now, things must be going OK.

The therapist disagrees. He says Manuela contacted him, that she's worried because for some time I've been acting strangely, the rest of my team hasn't been on board with my last few proposals, it's time for a status check.

While the therapist goes on about trivialities like personal decisions and emotional equilibrium and who knows what else, I realize that the responsible party, the reason I'm here putting up with this nonsense, is Roger. He must have written to Manuela, telling her he and the blonde don't endorse my latest ideas. The moment I put it together, I could've killed Roger, or at least screamed at him. Although that wouldn't help my case.

I practice diaphragmatic breathing, which I learned from the mindfulness teacher the therapist sent me to last time, and try to keep a peaceful look on my face. Certainly if I tell him I've just had the urge to hit my colleague, I'll have to waste even more time indulging this charade.

But it's hard to sustain abdominal breathing when I feel like breaking something. I try looking around to distract myself while I half listen. Suddenly everything seems too white, the sensation of peace I felt when I got here is gone. The patina on the desk we're sitting at blinds me, and I blink. The chairs are so pristine it's unnerving. Either no one has ever sat in them, or someone's obsessively cleaning them every five minutes.

Does the therapist himself do that? Does he clean chairs between consultations? Maybe he has a bottle of hydrogen peroxide somewhere. If you're really paying attention, it smells like antiseptic, not the reassuring freshness of a newly cleaned house, but something sharper, more penetrating.

"Let's get started, OK?" the therapist says.

I don't know why he asks. He knows as well as I do that I'm here due to a contractual obligation, that I have to answer his every question, do whatever he recommends. On that last point, the contract isn't entirely clear. If he told me to drink more wine, eat saturated fats, or dye my hair blonde, would I have to do it or risk being fired?

"OK," I say, in my neutral voice.

He looks at me over his glasses. He's been far-sighted for years, I remember he had the same ones last time I came here, he must be in his fifties, and suddenly I ask myself what a man his age could possibly know about my life. I try to restrain the thought. Like everyone else, he's been chosen by Manuela, so there must be something special about him.

"You seem a little preoccupied," he says with a kind smile. "Has something been bothering you?"

"No, nothing really."

"Take your time, María. I want you to really think about this."

Someone should have told him not to call me María, but even here, there's information that doesn't flow where it should.

"I go by Mary, actually."

"Of course." That inscrutable smile again. "So, Mary, tell me, what's on your mind these days? Anything that comes up for you is just fine."

"Well, I've been having these dreams about worms."

There it is, the first thing that comes out of me. His smile is clearly effective.

"Worms... how interesting. And what exactly happens with the worms?"

I start to sweat again. There's simply no way to stop it. I try the breathing technique, but no luck. The therapist just keeps looking at me, smiling indecipherably over his glasses, I notice my muscles relaxing, and then, without wanting to, I say:

"The worms devour us, Roger and me. Or we devour them, I'm not sure. I'd have no problem eating worms, to be honest, I know people eat them in many cultures, they're healthy, high in protein. I think I saw that in a documentary. I like watching documentaries before bed," I venture. "And as far as being eaten by worms, well, it doesn't sound great, but I could handle it."

I sweat, seas of sweat, the sweat drips down my forehead, my neck, my spine. There are stains forming around my armpits, and the more I try to stop, the more I sweat. What I'm unable to tolerate is the lack of definition. I try to distinguish what's happening, close my eyes, remember the dream, but it's impossible, I still don't know who's eating whom.

As if I'd shared the most mundane detail, the therapist says:

"Aha."

I say nothing, he waits for me to go on, but I'm empty of words. I'm enveloped in a sea of sweat and silence, warm but deadly, and I can't seem to get out.

"You mentioned Roger is with you in the dream. Why do you think that is?"

"Roger? Yes, well, of course he's there, we've been working together, the two of us, for a year now. More than a year. We're WhiteAngel, you've probably heard of us."

"Of course, WhiteAngel is an excellent team. But why do you think Roger shows up in your dream?"

"I told you. We work together."

"Nothing else?"

I look at him questioningly while the sweat continues dripping from my neck, my armpits, but I don't care anymore, it's like it's numbing me on its way out.

"Well, he was also my match for a while."

"Your match?"

Sometimes older people exasperate me, you have to explain the simplest things to them.

"Yes, my sexual partner."

"Sexual partner? You mean you were going out together?"

I almost laugh out loud.

"No, we weren't going out. He was just my match."

"Meaning?"

"We had sex with each other on Thursdays, to keep our neuro-transmitters at optimal levels."

I feel like I'm teaching a middle school class. Nothing about this consultation makes sense. The realization makes my muscles relax completely, and I stop sweating.

"I see. But you're speaking in the past tense, do you mean he's no longer your"—he hesitates—"match?"

"No, not anymore. Now his match is Helen, the newest member of WhiteAngel."

"I see."

The therapist writes something down in his notebook, I find it inconceivable that there are people still using notebooks.

"And how do you feel about that?"

"Feel? I don't feel anything about it. They're a good match, and Roger wasn't working for me anymore."

The therapist raises his eyebrows, he seems to be showing surprise, but again, it's hard for me to say, especially because his neutral smile comes right back.

"Wasn't working for you because . . ."

"Because of the worms, like I said. How could I sleep with someone who's being eaten by worms?"

"Of course, of course."

It seems there are no more questions. He looks at me, still smiling.

"OK, María." He retains nothing. "We'll call you."

I leave his office feeling I've done good work. It's shocking how many things I had to explain. I'm not putting Manuela on trial, by any means, but whatever skills the therapist has are very well concealed.

I got a nice yoga outfit for the relaxation sessions the therapist will probably recommend. Leggings, a top that isn't too tight but still shows your shape, in a color that's soothing enough, and a super-insulated, sweatproof yoga mat. But when I arrive at the office, the therapist gives me a funny look. I don't know what's gotten into him. He tells me we need to talk.

It feels strange to be here so early, rather than working at my own desk. The sun has just come up and the furniture, now that I look at it, isn't as white as it seemed last time, it has a slightly pink tone. The therapist also seems pink, maybe because he's so fair, he must have been blonde at some point. In the direct morning light—his office faces east, that's a perk for senior-level employees—his smile doesn't strike me as neutral anymore, there's something else behind it. A motive? Some level of discomfort?

"Sit down, please, María."

I don't tell him again that my name is Mary, he's obviously experiencing neural degeneration.

"How have your last seven days been?"

I guess we're on a coffee date now. That's not the approach I would take, but I'll play along if it ends in me getting my job back. Since I left, the blonde and Roger have gone up five points in value. It seems they've hit on yet another algorithm, though it's not live yet. I'm dying to try it out.

My week of "rest" has been a waste of time. Apart from finding the ideal yoga outfit, I mostly watched TV shows, which, beyond forty minutes a day, is madness, they're all the same, you think there's talent there, but no, it's pure artifice. Of course it is, they're actors.

Out of sheer boredom, I've eaten more than usual. I've gained at least five pounds, and the scale is off limits until next week.

But that isn't what Pinky is hoping to hear. I settle on, "Things are good, this week was just what I needed. I've rested, I've walked, I've eaten well. I'm feeling better already."

"Aha."

"I also bought some nice yoga gear."

"Why yoga gear, María?"

Each time he says María, I think of my grandmother on my dad's side: María, set the table. María, sit up straight. The woman only opened her mouth to criticize or give orders. It's better her generation is on its way out.

"Well, last time... I thought..."

"Yes?"

"I thought you'd recommend yoga and breathing exercises, that kind of thing, so I can get back to normal."

The moment this sentence is out of my mouth, I regret it.

"Because that's what you want, María? To get back to normal?"

"Yes, of course."

"But you know things change, don't you, María?"

There she is. I can hear her. My grandmother, telling me: "Why don't you take up those pants? You're walking all over them."

"Of course. Everyone knows that. It's the second law of thermodynamics: entropy increases."

"All right, yes. Let's work with that. You realize we can't go back to a prior state, don't you? No matter how much we might want to."

I'm amused when Pinky talks about physics. Droplets of sweat appear on his forehead, it's too much effort for him. Curiously, I'm sweating less. It's been three days since I've had to shower more than once in twenty-four hours.

"Well, no, of course not, all we can possibly do is achieve another state of equilibrium, with greater entropy than the one we were in before. Free ourselves up a little, at least."

Pinky frowns. As a senior-level employee, I may be obliged to attend these sessions—my junior contract didn't include that clause—but at least I can keep them interesting. There's nothing contractually preventing me from using scientific terms.

"Another state of equilibrium—see? I was hoping we'd get there."

The poor man has no idea what he's talking about. But I shouldn't be surprised. Back when he was in school, there wouldn't have been good data on emotional states. It was probably so long ago they were still teaching psychoanalysis or some similar concoction.

"That's what we need, María, another state of equilibrium."

I'm not making this easy, I know, but did he have to resort to "we"? Has he exhausted all other methods?

They make me do two more sessions while I'm on "well-earned

leave," as Pinky puts it. According to him, I've sacrificed a great deal for the company, and it's only right that they recognize it. Meanwhile, I've reorganized my apartment at least twenty times, and have also discovered the woman who cleans it is not as punctilious as I thought. There were substantial layers of dust and even dust bunnies behind the furniture and the picture frames, and under the bed, too. Did she think I wasn't going to look underneath my own bed? That's the last time I call her. Sometimes I don't understand people.

After the third session, Pinky accepts defeat. I've been explaining what entropy means, but he seems to understand nothing. He's looking at me sadly, or maybe he's frustrated, or angry, therapists try so hard to hide their emotions that they all end up looking the same.

"I think it's best if we carry on with our 'work,'" he's stuck on that word, with no idea what it means, "using another methodology. I wish you all the best, Mary."

Look at that, now he remembers. You have to laugh. Could he be in an early stage of dementia? Those holes, and then suddenly remembering something like that. It wouldn't surprise me.

The next morning, I have a message from Manuela. I'm so excited my palms start to sweat, like they did before college exams. Finally, back to work.

"Mary, I know you've made good progress with Tomás"—Pinky— "but I don't think the sessions with him are what you need right now." I concur. Manuela, you understand me. "I'm sending along a test that, in conjunction with our data, should give us a better idea of what to try next."

Data, a test. We're finally getting somewhere. It's not exactly what I was hoping for, but it's a start. Thank you, Manuela, for looking after us. Someone around here is thinking. I don't tell her that, of course. Just: "Yes, I'll send it back shortly. Thanks so much, as ever."

I would hug that woman, kiss her with tongue. It's a shame the main office is so far away, that she's always traveling. You can't catch her in the same city for more than two days at a time. But she's there for us when it counts. She's the light at the end of the tunnel.

How often do you feel like you've forgotten something?

Never

Rarely

Sometimes

Once a day

A few times a day

All the time

(My memory's great—how else could I do work like this?)

Rarely.

From one to one hundred, what number describes your degree of satisfaction with the company?

Ninety? (I don't want to seem like a workaholic.)

From one to one hundred, what number describes your degree of satisfaction with your life?

(With my life? Let's see. My apartment has a great view and very nice furniture, I paid for it in cash, I enjoy my work, eighty?) Eighty-three. (There are certainly areas for improvement, the flooring in the apartment, for example, and I should be exercising more, running, working out, I know, I know, but no one is perfect.)

If there's one thing in life you couldn't do without, what is it?

(Food? Water? I don't understand the question. I start to think Pinky made this test. Where's the rigor, the exactitude?)

Science.

How many times per day do you socialize with friends?

(All the time, I never stop socializing: every day I talk to Roger, well, not since the blonde arrived, but it's just a parenthesis. I talk to the people on other teams, we're always sending each other messages: How's it going? Amazing work! Check this out! And the Seattle team sends updates every week...)

Two to three.

How often do you go out with friends on the weekend?

(These questions are dated. People who go out have nothing better to do—go out where, to a movie? Shopping? Everything is online.)

Once. (At least once, with Roger. Well, not now, but that's going to change. Like I said, it's a parenthesis.)

From one to one hundred, please rate your emotional closeness with your family.

Fifty. (Like anyone who works, I'm not glued to my father all day, and even if I weren't working, to what end? I have no interest in selling figurines for kids' communions. Seeing him every two months is enough.)

From one to one hundred, please rate your emotional closeness with yourself.

(What? That's ridiculous. One hundred, like everyone else. Until we figure out cybernetic transmigration.)

Seventy-five.

If you had to do another kind of job, what would it be?

(Another kind of job? Are they trying to transfer me? No, that's impossible. Manuela said my profile was, and I quote, "ideal for this position, just what we need.")

Theoretical physicist.

What do you see yourself doing three decades from now?

Retired, in a beach house, taking care of my grandchildren.

Working, I like to stay ahead.

At home, surrounded by family.

At home, surrounded by friends.

With my companion animals, reading and resting.

(OK, it's prospective analysis. They don't want to know what I'm going to do in three decades, they just want to know what I can imagine doing, to then adjust my current job according to the data. Good, we're back on track.)

Working, I like to stay ahead.

How do you interpret the dream about the worms?

(So it's personalized. The conversations with Pinky weren't entirely pointless, then. I knew Manuela wouldn't have put him there for no reason. And it's an open-ended question, which means they'll have to contrast it against what's in thousands of databases. I like that. But how do I interpret it? Have I interpreted it at all? Calm down, breathe, everything can be solved with good data, good algorithms, just go with it. That's the smartest thing you can do.)

I think the worms represent what's inside of me, and the slime is the external world.

I go to bed without eating dinner. The responses to the questions filled me up. Not like if I had eaten, but mentally, on a neural level, a cellular level. That's what good therapy should do.

I'm tired but can't fall asleep. The slime and the worms are still there, even if at a distance. To distract myself, I imagine what it would be like to meet Manuela. I wish I could see her in person, even just once. Talk with her face to face.

I open my tablet and look at her profile. She has brown eyes, an unremarkable nose, neither large nor small, an unremarkable face, brown hair, medium length. But the look in her eyes mists over all her features: a wisdom that makes guessing her age impossible.

There's also some personal information, they ask us to fill it out so we can get to know each other. She likes to play Scrabble, likes ornamental plants. There's a photo of her garden. She has begonias, daisies, verbena, something I think is a kind of geranium, though its petals are smaller than usual. She could be anywhere in the Western world.

If we met, we would chat in her garden, wherever it is. She would tell me how to care for the plants, I'd listen very attentively—though I couldn't care less about plants—and we'd look at each other and feel understood.

Since I can't sleep, I start to imagine my responses being compared with thousands of others. Now with information emailed in by a researcher in Brazil, who also has dreams about worms, now with high-performing thirty-nine-year-old scientists born in Eastern countries, now with women who have college degrees and who, for no apparent reason, start sweating uncontrollably, now with the data of every 2003 physics graduate, independent of gender, now with a senior big data manager in Minneapolis who posted on social media seven months ago that she'd lost interest in sex for unknown reasons.

The idea of that data floating, arranging itself, and, finally, coalescing into answers puts me entirely at ease, and I fall asleep.

In the morning, I have a message from Manuela. That was quick, even by our standards, but I'm happy, I'm always happy to hear from her. No more fruitless therapy sessions, no more feeling around for answers in the dark.

Dear Mary:

Your test results are as follows:

In seventy percent of cases, subjects' experiences and progressions demonstrated a strong desire for another presence in their lives.

In ninety percent of cases involving subjects who identified as women, the solution was the decision to have children.

In the case of subjects who identified as male, sixty percent resolved their situations by deciding to have children, twenty percent by seeking out a legal union with another subject, and ten percent by acquiring objects with a value equal to or greater than their annual earnings.

For ten percent of male- and female-identified subjects, there was no data; it was omitted from calculations for unknown reasons.

I hope you find the study helpful. As you know, only you can decide what your next step should be. Until you do, I think it's wise for you to keep resting.

Hugs and kisses,

Manuela

Ten percent of the data was omitted? Why? Did those subjects all have terminal illnesses? I had a physical last month, everything was fine.

I thought once I got the data, I'd go back to sleeping perfectly. But insomnia has taken hold again, only now it's not the worms that keep me up, it's the ten percent. What could have happened to them? Every possibility seems awful, increasingly so as the night wears on.

Blasco • Diana

Everything that's not Laila is indecipherable now. I read the investment reports and don't understand them. It's as if I've forgotten why they exist, what you're supposed to do with them.

Each small detail of her body magnifies and fills my entire mind. Her legs, luminous and folded to one side—always the left—like those of a gentle animal. Her smooth neck, her chest, almost flat. Each one of her cells is awakening dormant memories, things I may not have lived but which feel like they happened yesterday.

If the withdrawal symptoms continue, soon it will become difficult to interact with clients. The complaints will roll in, and with them, more problems.

I must urgently come to my senses, and for that, I need my fix.

Diana is out with a friend from college. I take advantage of her absence to make a gin and tonic, she doesn't approve of my drinking midweek, then I open my computer. I hesitate for a moment before I press enter, and when I finally do, my entire body suffers an electric shock.

Laila's face shines in the pale light of an autumn afternoon—at least I know we're in the same hemisphere. She's still reading. She hasn't finished *The Stranger*. Her eyes follow the lines from one side to the other.

I come imagining Laila discovering first, pleasure, then pleasure's fatal attraction, and then, its implicit tragedy. That's enough, I barely need to touch myself.

I go to the next screen, and the next, and the next. She's shown nothing of her body except for incipient breasts that, now finishing the book, she grazes as she pulls down her shirt. A jolt of pleasure runs through us both, she moans lightly, I come again.

When Diana gets home, I'm in bed, awake but completely spent. Her cold body slides in next to mine, hugs me. It's pleasant, like a hug from a sibling.

Nothing can diminish the electricity of the night.

To keep seeing Laila, I'll require a prodigious sum of money, so I get back in the ring and schedule two early-morning meetings.

Everything goes well. The clients leave convinced that it's most advantageous to invest their savings in primary agricultural products in developing countries. That's the package we're selling this week, to the small and mid-level investors I work with. We have to put their money where the firm tells us to. But that's not all. They need to leave absolutely convinced that we're going to make them rich, and also that their investments are risk-free.

Of course, their investments come with many risks, but they're good for the firm, because to put it simply, the firm works on behalf of the biggest accounts, period. If the microeconomy thrives, the macroeconomy suffers: it's one of the first things they teach you. Even after all these years, it's hard for me to believe people don't catch on.

Our work doesn't end there, either. The hardest thing is convincing them, when the returns are negative—two in every three cases—that it's wisest to keep investing.

We're tasked with turning our clients into gamblers.

And to do that, you have to get them to stop making calculations. Rather, they need to "follow their instincts," "go on their nerve." Our expensive suits, our elegant ties, the consultants' fine gold chains and subtle, effective makeup, the furniture we update every year, the neutral shades of paint, always that color you wear no matter the season, are no more than a guise to convince the clients they've stepped into a place of public service instead of a casino.

We're the casino escort. The one who encourages you to keep playing, keep losing, but always with a smile on her face, and a silken voice that envelops you and convinces you the next trump card will be yours.

Of course, the house always wins.

The uninsured investments lay the foundation for the insured ones, it's that simple.

My awareness of all this has, from time to time, paralyzed me, and that's one reason why our team lead has it in for me. Today, though, I feel sure I could convince anyone of anything.

Lunchtime arrives and my euphoria is still intact, so I tell them to send me a Classified. That's what we call small investors who've lost a substantial part of their earnings and have yet to be informed.

Although there's a bonus involved, no one wants them, because often they make a scene. That money was for their retirement, their kids' college fund, their only grandchild, who was left all alone when the parents died in a car crash... They simply can't believe it, *you have to do something to fix this, give us back our savings, we don't care about returns, just give us what we put down at the start.*

Well, you should have thought of that sooner, you want to say. But that's not how it's done. You have to weave a convincing story, and preferably, keep them from cashing out what little is left, because if they stay with us, there's opportunity. That sort of thing.

Our team lead looks surprised but agrees immediately. People get put in that job for their instincts, or at least that's what they say, who knows what really goes on in HR. Diana refused to disclose anything even to me when she was team lead, although I guess that's one reason they chose her for the role.

It goes better than expected. The profits were supposed to go toward a beach house. He could have afforded a small one, but that wasn't enough—he wanted something extravagant, where he could host his work friends, now also retired, to inspire a certain envy. Something to sweeten old age. It's not hard for me to convince him to stay with us. There will never be enough money if it's just sitting at the bank, not for the big house but not for the small one he could have afforded either, so therefore, there's nothing to lose. That last bit of the argument does the trick, he looks calmer, repeating again and again that it's for the best. It's a lie, of course: there's always more to lose.

When we say goodbye, he squeezes my hands for a long time, he's sincere. It's incredible how much sincere hand-squeezing happens in these offices. And sincere on all sides, too—at least for an instant. During that brief interval when the two bodies are touching, both believe they're doing what's best for everyone. Bodies can't lie to each other. But as soon as the hand-squeezing finishes, we go back to not believing: calculations invade and impose their order on everything.

The team lead is keeping an eye on me. He doesn't trust me. My accounts are doing worse than they were last fiscal year. Not embarrassingly bad, but worse than before, and it's his job to notice that kind of thing.

He calls me to his office:

"B"—he calls me "B" when he's in a good mood—"I'm impressed. You handled that well. Would you like to work with more Classifieds?"

That's the team lead's job, keeping an eye out for winning streaks and finding a way to capitalize, like someone who's found the mother lode. You have to dig until it's gone, dig fast; stay ahead of collapses, poisonous gases, and floods.

"Well, that depends."

He frowns. He wasn't expecting resistance. But he doesn't turn me away. He knows it's rare for the stars to align, and you have to make the most of it when they do.

"All right. I'll get back to you with a number."

A number. That's exactly what I need.

If I can maintain a pace of two Classifieds per day, I'll have the money I need in two months.

Getting the money is my only option. I'm no longer able to access Laila's profile. The last time I tried, a banner appeared: "We know what you want. To take the next step, write to xxx.com." So I wrote to them, and they sent me a PDF with full instructions: Laila feels the same way I do, she wants to meet me, but she lives far away—they don't say where—and needs money for travel expenses, preparations, and clothes.

I concentrate on the numbers. My heart shouts win, win, win! and I know I will. The phone rings again and again, but I don't pick up. I won't permit any distractions.

Suddenly a hand on my shoulder breaks my trance. It's Diana, she gestures for me to follow her to her office.

"Blasco, will you explain yourself please?"

The room, with its huge window facing the courtyard and its traces of high-end air freshener, instantly seems as strange to me as Diana does. I look at it all like I'm seeing it for the first time as my wife carries on, trying not to shout but barely succeeding.

"So first you empty the accounts, and now you're putting in money like we're saving for a Porsche."

I'm unable to say anything, can suddenly only marvel that the body before me, for which I feel nothing more than a slight compassion, belongs to the person with whom I've spent the last ten years of my life.

"Look, you can tell me now, or I can follow the money. Whatever you prefer."

She's sitting on the leather sofa we picked out together years ago, when the future still seemed like a luminous territory, full of surprise and adventure.

I review the lies I could tell. I'm about to say I'm addicted to gambling, poker, something honorable. Instead, I say:

"I'm addicted to a porn. I'm in love."

Diana looks more surprised than angry and tells me to go back to my office, we'll talk later.

But that night she doesn't say a word to me. She eats a sandwich in front of the TV and goes to sleep.

My wife crawls into the lap of her sleeping pills, and I don't dare get in bed. I wander around the house, from the living room to the study, checking my phone over and over. Xxx.com has notified me that Laila has had a minor setback and will require an additional sum, which I can't deposit now, because after our conversation this morning, Diana locked the accounts.

Without money, there are no messages.

I dwell on my rage at the people running the site and make one coffee after another, I don't want to sleep in case Laila writes. I'm sure she'll find a way to circumvent their policy and contact me.

Diana wakes up almost happy. She makes toast for us both and has a leisurely breakfast, reading the news on her tablet.

On our way to work, she barely talks, a comment about the central bank's upcoming credit check, about how it could affect our investments—by "ours," she means the company's—the usual.

I cancel the morning's two Classifieds, lacking the strength to bear witness to tears. I turn on my computer and act as though I'm working while mentally I return to the calculations that have been ripening for the last week. Something's not adding up. I don't know how I thought I could make the money Laila and I need so quickly.

I try to grab on to the memory of her to avoid losing my footing, because I've started to feel the floor lurching beneath me. I'm careening toward an abyss. But her dazzling skin is losing its shine, and her dark eyes, steady, absolute, seem lighter, maybe a hint of brown, maybe some glint that seems out of place, as if she's really just sixteen years old like they claim.

I should kneel at my wife's feet—she didn't report me for buying what they're selling as child pornography, nor did she ask for a divorce, and she kept me from getting fired. But instead, I'm staring at her like a fool, incapable of forming any one facial expression.

Diana isn't surprised. At this point, she expects little of me. She just says, "We're going to get through this. It's just a rough patch, every couple has them. We're going to get you help."

We eat in silence, salad and toast with salmon. And that's how it begins, what Diana christens "our new life." This new life, I learn in the days that follow, is going to be "very blessed," because "the crisis we're facing will help us grow together," and to celebrate our good luck, Diana makes an appointment at the fertility clinic, and I say that's a great idea, just what we need.

Angélica • Carlos • Diana • María

What am I doing? That's what I've been asking myself since Carlos cornered me on the rooftop, waiting for me to say something, and all I managed was, "Could you back up please? I'm scared of heights." *What am I doing* is all I can think while I'm studying Hester's notebook, which is now in my bag at all times.

I know Carlos is still waiting for my answer, he's very single-minded. But it's like there's just silence inside me, no instincts, just a vision of life as a puzzle I need to solve, with some pieces missing. I have pieces, but they don't fit anywhere. So I concentrate on couple 1156 and hope that if I pay attention to what I do know, things will somehow be returned to their former harmony.

Today is their fourth attempt.

At first, Diana, the wife, would say she wanted a boy. That's not rare with moms—they're likely thinking men have fewer problems. She stopped saying anything like that after the second round. Now she'll just be happy if it works.

"See, Diana? Quick and painless," Lisa says as she inserts the needle.

Diana tries to smile. I feel a little sorry for her, she looks like she's not doing well, though she's trying to hide her exhaustion with perfect hair, brown with golden highlights, and peach-colored blush.

The husband doesn't talk much, just holds his wife's hand. He knows it's all up to fate now.

We can't tell them—it's against company policy—but their case is more complicated than most. Both are over forty, and they aren't taking sperm from donors. So they're working with less than ideal raw materials.

Over the last four months, Lisa and I have watched them move from one emotional state to the next, unable to do much to stop it. Our role—this, they've made very clear to us, in training and the handbook—is to support them throughout the process, offering "positive, hopeful" phrases. The board is convinced a depressive environment will lower our success rate. There's no study to back that up, but the thinking is, it can't hurt.

1156 has been through every phase.

That first round, they were hopeful.

"We haven't slept in two days," she said.

They were grinning like a new couple. He looked a little sheepish and added, "That probably seems crazy. But sleep is the last thing on my mind right now."

When they showed up for the third attempt, they were still in good spirits.

"Three rounds is normal at our age, right?" she asked.

"Oh, absolutely," said Lisa, who handles these situations much better than I do. "Completely normal."

"There are three playgrounds in our neighborhood," the husband said while we proceeded with the procedure. "I never noticed that before. It's incredible."

Lisa and I nodded to signal that yes, it was incredible. And I felt a twinge of anguish thinking that the life they were already building might never belong to them.

She'd probably decided where they would send the child for school, even who they would call to babysit when they had some obligation. As someone who worked in finance, she must have had the money sorted too. A separate account for college tuition, maybe some cash put aside for a move, since their current apartment—they lived in the city center, in an ungentrified area—wasn't great for kids.

After that, the husband stopped speaking. He just squeezed Diana's hand and tried to display a comforting smile. The fortitude of those first few days was totally depleted.

Though he'd hidden it well at the early appointments, the husband couldn't help but try to distract himself. Several times I caught him sneaking glances at Lisa, and, at least once, at my hips.

But eventually, even those signs of life disappeared completely. His appearance had changed, his eyes had lost that hard mineral shine. I'd say he'd even gained a few pounds. His body was adapting to the rhythm of the wait.

The way the two of them were looking—ready to live their "parenthood project," as they were calling it—it seemed likely that after the fourth failed attempt, they would finally accept semen from a donor, and maybe with that plus the arrival of spring—in March, the success rates are higher—we would finally get results.

Carlos comes over. I told him I'm exhausted from case 1156, but instead of letting me rest, he insisted on keeping me company.

We order Indian food.

"First spicy food, then spicy sex," he says, half joking and half serious.

It's the kind of comment I found endearing at first, the kind that made our life seem like one big adventure, but with every repetition, that image has dimmed, and now it's a life like any other, the life of the girl in the last commercial you saw.

"What are you doing?" I ask myself again. While out loud, I can only muster, "OK."

Which really doesn't mean anything, which is the worst thing you can do. Mean nothing.

We eat in silence. Carlos has insisted we sit at the dining room table instead of on the couch as usual. So we've transferred the food to plates: rice and lamb curry on a platter, raita in one bowl and mint chutney in another.

Carlos wolfs down the lamb and rice while I focus on spreading a little mint chutney on some naan. Naan tastes like burlap to me, not that I've ever tried burlap, but I imagine it feels the same way on the palate, rough and dry.

"You're the best thing that's ever happened to me," Carlos says.

He looks into my eyes and raises a glass of Sauvignon Blanc, which, it seems, is the recommended pairing for Indian food.

I look back at him and think about how far this is from my idea of rest, and suddenly I remember one Friday night when we met up with his coworkers at a cocktail bar they go to after work. The place is lit up in metallic tones, oranges and indigos, and under the bar there's a blue fluorescent light and red velvet chairs. At first it seems loud, almost tasteless, but around the time you go for your second drink, it starts to make sense.

"This is my pretty lady friend," he said when he introduced me. "Who needs Jennifer Lawrence? And she's smart too. Don't get any ideas."

His colleagues laughed. They were used to his delivery, always jovial, half-ironic. Then they talked about global finance.

They speculated another full-blown crisis was on the way, which, judging by their laughter, made them almost giddy. It wasn't clear if the cause of the laughter was the crisis itself or the fact that they could predict it, or maybe the knowledge that international economic order was irremediably fucked.

I observed their white teeth, listened to their laughter, which seemed synchronized, and understood that, cynical as they were, they'd been granted a sense of belonging I would never understand.

That night I wanted to be the person Carlos had described, his very own Jennifer Lawrence, and for a minute, I think I turned into her, behaved as she would have behaved, was resonant but light.

I bring the glass of wine to my lips and drink, waiting for a phrase to come to me and solve everything. But in my mind, there's just that humming. What are you doing? I drink. The liquid tastes like cherries, apples, wood, everything but wine, and I smile.

Since the night we had Indian food, we've done nothing but wander around the city. People sit chatting on patios. With propane heaters, it's nice sitting outside, since the cold is already letting up. There's a growing crowd carrying shopping bags, all looking very determined, as if they're on an important mission. It's the new spirit of spring.

We're back at my house. Before, Carlos had more than enough enthusiasm for both of us when it came to realizing plans from the Sunday supplement, and we'd go to movies, or eat cake at a trendy new bakery.

We get in bed and try to fuck. We touch each other, get close, repeat the gestures that worked until now.

"I don't know what's going on with me," Carlos says, pulling away a little.

For days he hasn't been able to get it up.

I stroke him a little and he seems to respond, then I get on top of him, shirt on, underwear off. That used to drive him crazy. Nothing.

He says he doesn't feel well. He goes to get a cigarette and smokes it out the window. A little smoke gets in anyway, and I cover my mouth with the comforter to avoid breathing it in.

He comes back to bed and hugs me.

"Don't worry," I say. "It happens."

He doesn't seem to hear me, just sits quietly for a minute then says, "OK."

"OK?"

"Tomorrow I'm going to donate."

Early on, I had insisted he consider it, we can never have too many quality donors. But then I stopped bringing it up. Why that now, all of a sudden?

At eleven in the morning, I get a text: "All done, three containers, just for your VIP clients." He sends a photo of the containers, tagged and ready to go in the freezer.

Lisa and I are preparing to meet with 1156. In cases like these, you're supposed to "be honest, but keep things open-ended." We'll have to present them with next steps: potentially, the use of donated semen, or better yet, donated embryos. This is the hard part, I need to focus.

But I've already opened Carlos's message and he's waiting for a reply, so I send back a smiley face emoji. I immediately regret it and briefly consider unsending it, but that would be even worse. I leave it there.

Today the clinic smells especially aseptic. They deep clean it every night, and to hide the chemical odor, they use special air-freshener in the ducts. It makes me think of a perfumed rat, I can stomach it less each day. People have the idea that a sanitized place will smell good, but it's just the opposite. It smells like death.

There are mornings, like this one, when I want to put on a face mask. The only thing that gives me any relief is Lisa's presence. Her body, which always gives off a fresh, slightly sweet scent, seems to cleanse the air.

We make a list, discuss the options, and decide we'll advocate for going straight to embryos. We agree that Lisa will give them the bad news, console them, and offer them a way forward. They're going to resist, and that's where I'll come in, there's no other option, to convince them that "we're one hundred percent with you on your parenthood project," and that the success rate is much higher with donated embryos.

Ten minutes before the appointment, we get lab results.

"Diana, you're pregnant."

Lisa can't hide the emotion in her voice.

They weren't expecting that: he'd come in with his head down, like a cow on its way to the slaughterhouse; she couldn't stop twisting her wedding ring, trying to hold back tears.

We explain that we'll need to confirm the results with an ultrasound. They agree. They're moving more slowly now, as if they've collided with something and their bodies aren't taking it well.

We place the transducer inside her, and the image appears on the monitor. The husband looks at it, disconcerted, while he squeezes his wife's hand. This time she's the one holding him up.

The results of the ultrasound are surprising. The embryo is larger than it should be. I look at Lisa, who has already realized. The couple is stunned by the sound, and the image the monitor casts: you can already make out the head, the torso, the tiny extremities.

I tell them we want to give them a moment, and Lisa and I step outside the exam room and into the office.

"Is it a defect?" she asks. She's still convinced I always have the answers.

"Wait," I say. "Let's look again."

We review the digital versions. There's no indication of abnormality. Then it hits me.

"It's not the husband's."

"What?" Lisa says. "But..."

"There's no way around it. Look. The last insemination was five weeks ago, right?"

"Right."

"But this embryo looks closer to nine weeks."

"But it could still be the husband's. I mean, maybe they, maybe it happened... naturally."

"Look at the husband's semen analysis."

"Right, right. It can't be his."

We go back to the exam room and let the wife know we'll need to do one more test. She smiles, trying to hide her fear. You can tell that's how she responds to adverse circumstances: that smile is probably her most effective weapon at work, she's used to giving orders and sharing bad news. Her husband, however, is immune to her charms. Husbands become immunized, I've seen it again and again. It's a way of surviving, I guess.

We explain that for this test, she'll need to come back with us alone, since there's some radiation involved, but not to worry, exposure is minimal. It's one of the tricks we use when we need to separate couples.

She's so far gone she doesn't ask what kind of test. We guide her to a meeting room.

"Sit down, Diana," I say.

She immediately does.

"So, you're pregnant, but according to our analysis, the pregnancy happened before your last appointment. Is it possible the pregnancy happened naturally?"

Lisa is next to me but in the background, so we won't intimidate her. Diana looks first at me then at Lisa, but her expression is blank. She must be overwhelmed. A few seconds pass, and she says, "It's possible."

I'm not sure she's understood, so I insist. She's now twisting her ring again, as if she's casting a spell, and I get the sense she's very far away.

"Diana, what I'm saying is, it's impossible that your embryo was produced here at the clinic."

She looks at Lisa, then at me. I gesture to Lisa to bring her in.

"The probability that it's your husband's," my colleague says—she's trying to keep her voice as neutral as possible—"keeping in mind the quality of his untreated semen, is almost zero. Of course, if you'd like confirmation, we could always do a prenatal paternity test."

It's a trick they teach us when we join the Plant: "Communicate everything in the same voice you'd use to recite the periodic table."

Diana looks at the two of us again, but her eyes settle on Lisa. It's clear that's who she has chosen as her interlocutor.

"No, that won't be necessary. Thanks for letting me know," she says. Her voice doesn't even waver.

We go back to the exam room, where the husband is waiting. They hug.

"Didn't hurt a bit," Diana says.

On my way home, I can't stop thinking about what happened at the clinic. My metro car is packed. With the morning I had, I completely forgot it's better to wait until seven, though then you obviously get back later. There are so many of us it's impossible not to be touching another person.

I remember the notebook and start to panic. With my bag against my chest, maneuvering around the arm of an unmoving teen in headphones, I'm just able to reach one hand in and touch the cover.

Carlos comes over for dinner. He insisted, and although I'm completely drained, I couldn't say no.

"Look, Angélica," he says as soon as the door shuts behind him, while I'm filling two glasses of wine in hopes that alcohol will make things easier. "Life is simple. You either have them, or wish you did."

Everyone has heard that, but he delivers it like he's enlightening me. I start to suspect something is off.

Almost without touching the glass, he comes toward me and tries to tear off my shirt. Two of the buttons pop off. He acts like we're in a sex scene out of a movie, one where the lovers are almost violent, as if they want to kill each other.

I try to react, but my brain is asleep. Carlos tears off my tights and penetrates me. Two thrusts in, he goes soft.

His face darkens. The bravado is gone. I think he might cry or ask for forgiveness. I tell him he should leave.

I sit on the bed and wait for the door to slam shut. I bend to pick up the torn tights, which are bunched on the floor, and am overwhelmed with anger at having lost an object so useful and durable.

Then I realize my boyfriend's semen is frozen in a jar at my office, and that he'll probably never get hard with me again. My mind returns to 1156, our only success in the last several months, cause unknown. I think all this together must mean something, I just can't figure out what.

Maybe Hume was right and the law of causality is nothing more than wishful thinking, a way of making life tolerable, so we don't have to spend every second wondering what's coming next. So we can pretend we know what's coming next. Maybe the regional director isn't ignorant after all, maybe she's just more evolved than the rest of us, living in a state in which science no longer exists, isn't even a possibility. All that exists is a profit rate, growing or falling.

I shower. I put clean sheets on my bed, and before switching off the light on my nightstand, I write in Hester's notebook: "Couple 1156. 42. Uncertain."

Since I broke things off with Carlos fifteen days ago, Hester's notebook has been my only companion.

Its cover looks more and more worn, because I take it everywhere with me. In the morning I toss it in my bag, and as soon as I get to the office, I put it in the top desk drawer to keep it close. Whenever possible, I send Lisa off to do something—confirm an appointment, go for a bottle of water—then take out the notebook and scan its contents. The embossed lettering on the cover—"The Plant, where happiness is made"—continues to lose its luster.

At night, when I get home, I take it out, and if a case has been resolved, I make a note. That's now my evening ritual. I pour myself a glass of white wine, have a little cheese—I don't like to eat much at night—open it up, and read it intently. Since Diana, we've had no positive outcomes.

The pages are starting to yellow, and many nights I think it would be smart to make a scan, but I'm afraid of putting anything on the computer. Hacking keeps showing up in the news, everyone's hard drives seem vulnerable. They're usually looking for bank account passwords, but you can never be too safe.

Maybe because it's been fifteen days since Carlos, or maybe because I had too much wine last night, this morning, there's a strangeness to the way everything is unfolding. I've read this sometimes happens when your life is on the verge of changing abruptly, like you can sense it. Although it could also just be the hangover.

A VIP client is coming in today. She had her eggs frozen years ago—her company pays for the whole procedure. The moment she walks through the door, she says:

"Hello, good morning, I'm María Lebrel." She seems unusually sturdy, resolved, as if she's just here to get waxed or have her hair colored.

We tell her to sit down and explain the embryo transfer process. She listens closely, a little impatiently.

We begin the procedure.

Suddenly I remember the test tubes of semen, and I'm struck by the feeling that something is speeding up or going too slowly, as if our movements are no longer synchronized with time. I try to shake off the feeling. It's important to concentrate in these moments.

I look up at the ultrasound and am struck by the certainty that the semen used to fertilize the egg belonged to Carlos. I memorize the embryo ID number and keep going. My movements seem increasingly slow, my forehead and chest start to sweat. I'm afraid María will notice. I look at her and smile—they always say you should at this point in the procedure. But she's completely oblivious, her face shows no signs of discomfort.

Lisa makes sure the procedure is carried out flawlessly, her eyes dart back and forth, from the culture dish, to the ultrasound, to the monitor where we track María's vitals, to my hands. She doesn't seem to notice anything either.

When we finish, María dresses and says, "What are the odds it works the first time?" That same resolve in her voice.

"That depends on a lot of things, but you have an excellent shot, since we're using frozen eggs and high-quality sperm."

My response doesn't seem to convince her. She squints like she's making complex calculations, then she says, "When will I know if it worked?"

"It's best to wait a minimum of four weeks. On your way out, the front desk can schedule your next appointment."

"Four weeks," she murmurs, a shadow of disappointment on her face. She seems like the kind of person who, when she wants something, wants it now. She and Carlos would have been a good match.

When I get home, I compare the ID number in the picture Carlos texted against the clinic's records. Indeed, it was his sperm. I hesitate for a second, unsure what to do, and then I take out the notebook and put it on the table.

"Better not to drink today," I think. I start paging through it, as always. I've done it so many times there are sections I've almost memorized. I count up failures, successes.

I take out an A4 sheet and start tracing the general trends, month after month. Inseminations in green, failures in red, successes in blue. Again, the curves dance apart over time: the green and red ascending, the blue descending. I stare at them while I open a bottle. "One glass won't hurt," I think.

I rush the wine while I look at the graph and gradually become conscious of the noises in the street, the cars that stop at the light near the building then accelerate again, a driver honking, techno music blaring from someone's open window. I decided to live in Zone 3 because it was in my budget, but also because it's quiet. I could have found something smaller in Zone 4, but it would have been close to the highway, and there, you can't escape the noise of traffic. At least here, at night, things slow down, you can almost forget the daytime rush.

I tear up the A4 sheet and scatter the pieces between my recycling and my trash can. A security measure, probably pointless, but it makes me feel better anyway.

Up until today, I've drawn countless graphs: the success rate among older single women, younger single women, young couples, couples where the wife is younger than the husband... Every single time, I get a descending curve.

I don't know why I keep making graphs, what I'm hoping to find. Something that's not in the numbers, I think. Maybe I'm looking for meaning: in the plummeting curve, in my reality. Or maybe I'm looking for Hester, to feel, even if briefly, that someone is there on the other side.

Carlos

Yesterday I saw Coach. The guy is kind of a creep. For one thing, his mustache is bad, and not in the stylish way, or the ironic way, or the gay way, it's just bad. Like something straight out of the fifties. Makes me uncomfortable.

And you should see the way he walks around his living room—who the fuck puts on an act like that in his own living room—like he has the whole world at his feet. He's worse than me. And then all that crap about feeling your energy flowing, listening to your true self.

He gave me some pamphlet I shoved in my jacket pocket, thinking I'd toss it the second I stepped outside. But then I forgot. The only thing on my mind was getting out of there, fast.

When I get up, the pamphlet is out on the kitchen counter. No idea how it got there. I'm so hungover all I can do is sip water. It's delicious. Sometimes bland is best.

"Today is the first day of the rest of your life. Who do you want to be? How can you make it happen? Start now." The words are still crashing around in my head. The whole group said them together to close out the session, everyone totally straight-faced, looking infinity dead in the eye. At the time I thought it was stupid, but this morning it might be growing on me.

Right now my problems have more to do with the past than they do with the future. Where was I last night? Things start to get blurry right around three in the morning. Did I come home alone? Did I open the door? I have no way of knowing. Maybe it doesn't matter. The past is the past, right? That's the point. Get over it.

Overcome it.

Do whatever you have to do, but overcome it.

They haven't actually said that yet, but I'm sure it will come up in some later session. Isn't that the whole point?

On a day like this, I would usually call Diana. I like her to keep me company when I'm hungover. She sits on the couch and watches TV with me and waits. She's the one who sent me to Coach. She's worried about me. I think if I told her to leave her husband for me, she would.

I've never understood what Diana is doing with Blasco. The woman is sharp, she manages all the investments, national, international, and he's just like a ghost, the guy you work with for years and then see at a party and his face rings a bell, but you don't know why.

We'd go from the couch to the bed as quickly as possible. Diana is hot. She smells good, she takes smelling good very seriously—body wash, perfume. That's why I like her, and it's also why I haven't told her to leave her husband. Her perfume gets in the way.

Once we got there, I'd let her take charge. Hangovers destroy me and she knows it, she would get on top. She would come with a little scream, that scream that still throws me off, since it's not what you'd expect of someone whose mere presence keeps a hundred employees in line. She would tousle my hair and leave.

But I'm too afraid to call her, because I don't know if I'll be able to get it up, so I order a pizza and sink into the couch and watch TV.

When I wake up it's early morning, cool for April, but I'm sweating buckets. I change shirts and try to fall back asleep but can't.

I shower and attempt to piece things together. "Today is the first day of the rest of your life," I repeat.

Yeah, OK, but what do I do with that?

"How do you spell it, sir?"

Here we go again. I want to say, "Take a guess, asshole."

Starts with G. Sound it out.

My name is Gracias. Carlos Gracias.

There was a time when I thought about changing it. It's basically García. But I never got that far. Eventually, everyone would have found out. Just thinking about how annoying my sister would be about it made me feel uninspired. I don't get why you have to be so dramatic. You're so selfish. Did you even think about Mom, how she might feel about this? As if she gives a shit about our mom. It's not her last name anyway. And then, same old story, she starts crying. You need help. You're not OK. You're acting like this because of unresolved trauma. No, definitely not worth it.

I fill out the forms as quick as I can and leave.

I've always hated bureaucracy. Endless data-dealing, one place to another, one paper to the next. When I put my name down on any form, any official letter, I have the feeling I'm handing over a little piece of myself. But this time, it's actually worth it. This is the knockout punch that's going to break my losing streak. I've checked against all the data, it's a sure thing.

The woman behind the desk gives me a look that means I don't know what.

She's not bad.

A little fake, maybe because of the Botox. But for one night? Women in admin are good for one night. After that, they start to go on and on about things, interior design, gastronomy, international finance. As if they know what they're talking about.

It's a no, a definite no. No messing around today.

Well, it's done. The shake-up that's going to save me. I can feel it.

I almost turn back as I'm leaving the office. Her ass was nice, undeniably nice. But it's not worth it. Gracias, not today.

It could have been worse: my last name could have been No Gracias. Just like that, I'm back. Laughing at my own jokes.

"You know what your problem is?" People love saying that. And what's worse is, they really believe they have the answer. "Your problem is, you only know how to laugh at your own jokes." I have to admit that one hurt. Angélica, before leaving me.

It's not that I was offended. I'm not that type. No, it hurt because it was the last second of hope. A little voice inside said, if she's this mad, she must care. But it wasn't that, she had just gotten bored. "You're a lost cause," she said. She meant it.

Lost cause, lost boy, paradise lost. It's all in the eye of the beholder. It's the first day of the rest of my life. That's cause for celebration. I call Mario.

Alcohol's fine if you know how to handle it. On the fifth drink, the universe makes sense. You know it's fake. You know it's fleeting.

But it makes sense, and there you are: a lost boy in paradise lost, lost and found. Everything forgotten, everything no one's keeping an eye on, everything that stops mattering for a second but is then classified, ordered, described, numbered. Destroyed. A swing and a miss.

"You're hilarious, Carlos. Let's go."

We head down Calle de Victoria. Victory, why not.

There were others—years ago, centuries even—who lived and drank like us, who claimed victory.

"You want to hear something crazy?" I say.

We must sound ridiculous, now, from the outside. All those hours at the library together, inhuman drinking, the feeling that heaven was within reach. At night in the city. For us.

"I made an incredible investment," I say. "I signed this morning. It's foolproof."

"Of course it is," Mario says, "As long as I've known you, you've been coming out ahead."

"Impossible. Lisa, the brunette with those perfect curls."

"The very same," Coach says.

What a dog, he's fucking the brunette. Of course he passed on the skinny blonde.

I'm beginning to find him absolutely intolerable—the nerve—when the guy starts to cry right in front of me. Fuck, really? He's crying? Isn't his thing that he has it all figured out?

Really, it's my fault. I was the one who asked if he wanted to stay out. The others left a while ago, to avoid throwing the week off balance, or whatever. But I wasn't strong enough, I saw that gleam in his eye and thought: this guy will sign up for anything. Sure, he acts like an athlete—if you just reduce your carb intake, if you do a little yoga before breakfast—but he's been knocking them back all night. No one else even noticed. I'd bet my life that not one of them has shown up at work after pulling an all-nighter, probably no one has even smoked weed. They're the good kids, good workers, good chosen ones, good at being broken and put back together piece by piece.

And here we are. Just look at him. He must have been on the wagon, and that'll wreak havoc on anyone. With drinking, you have to be consistent.

Now, the two of us out and going shot for shot, I can see he's a regular con man, who would have thought. Drink is demanding, like a girlfriend—if you neglect her, she'll make you pay. That's the truth. Tears stream down his face. And yeah, for sure, the one with curly hair is hot. There's no way he was going for the blonde. Elena, Malena? Lately I've been terrible with names. That's another reason why they demoted me, probably. I look at those rich-ass faces and think, Pepe Alcaraz? Mario Segurada? Antolín Pazos? They all look the same to me, I've met with them twenty times each, but they're such dickheads I barely see them. And they're just waiting for me to slip up. But I can't help it, the names don't stick. And I'm all, *our pleasure, just say the word, whatever you need,* but that doesn't do it. Obviously, sooner or later, they realize. They're too much. Used to us knowing their birthdays, their anniversaries, girlfriends' names. We even call whatever whore they come in with by name. They're not your average whores, these ones are quality.

So the day's Alcaraz or Segurada complains. Naturally, he doesn't mention the name thing. He says something like, "Communication isn't quite what I was hoping for, I'm certain there's someone else who would be a better fit." So it goes, again and again, until management is onto you.

"Life is a scam," I say.

"No, Carlos. No. You can't think that way."

He comes over and hugs me. He's so sloshed he gets drool on my blazer. I should have changed before today's session, the last thing

I need is gunk on my jacket. Bespoke, sure, but covered in who knows what. "We're not going to tell you how to dress." The HR director who led the mini-course "Welcome to the Investment for Life Community" had a friendly voice, a smiling voice. "We simply want you to consider the image you're presenting to the client. Put yourself in the client's shoes—what would you be hoping to see? Apart from that, do as you like. We want you to feel comfortable with every part of your work life, from what you wear, to the way you schedule your projects. We want Investment to feel like home." And that's how all the newbies ended up spending their first three paychecks on designer clothes in which to feel "comfortable and genuine," courteous, always smiling, and shirts that cost enough to feed a family of four for a week.

I try to pull back a little, to see if the blazer is salvageable. He resists.

"Everything has meaning," he repeats. "It's there, you just have to know how to listen."

I don't agree or disagree. I peel him off me and order another whiskey. We're at the point of no return. He doesn't know because he's out of practice, but I do.

"Right," I finally say. "Everything has its meaning, and at the bottom of this glass, we're going to find it."

I've flirted with other drinks, gin and tonics and that kind of crap, but you always go back to the basics, what's right is right. With the perfect drink in you, nothing matters: not the brunette, not genetic recombination, not the boss slapping shoulders with everyone but me, not the feeling that we've lost big.

"She went off with a woman, Carlos."

"Who?" I ask.

"Lisa, Lisa, who else."

Ah, fuck, the curly-haired one. This many drinks in, it seems simply unreal that she's still on his mind. I pat him on the back, the worst of it seems to pass. It's not the place or time to feel bad for yourself. It's six in the morning, and we're at a sad excuse for a speakeasy in the basement of a music association. This is what it's come to ever since they mandated 2 a.m. bar close. It smells damp, like feet, and everyone's smoking. We're already breaking the rules, why not one more? If we were seeing straight, we'd have left by now.

"A woman?" I ask, once he's recovered. "You mean she left you for a woman?"

"No, she didn't leave me, we're still together. But she's also sleeping with her."

What a gal. I didn't see that coming. Now that we've gotten this far, I don't really know what to say to him. There's a jackass who's been circling us, I think he's selling coke, though it could be anything. He's a little cross-eyed. The kind of person who was fucked right out of the gate. Nobody would have hired him, not with a hundred master's degrees, so he opted for the middle way. Good for him.

I come back with half a gram and grab Coach's arm. He vacuums it up like nobody's business. The second line brings him right back to life.

"Let's go," he says.

Fighting words. He's gone overboard, he's in worse shape than me, the man has got it bad. He goes out to the dance floor again. I'm not big on keeping people in line. Normally it's reversed, so I rarely get to practice. With the pseudo clarity from that last line, I decide I'll join him.

The dance floor is full of zombies. There are a bunch of guys who look like they've just hit forty. I'd bet half of them have wives, kids too, and here they are putting it all on the line. The others aren't fit to play. They're all missing something, too tall, too short, or their noses are ugly, or something worse, something you can't detect just by looking, and they're out burning up their last hopes. The whole scene makes me want to hug them and call them "brother." There are very few women. They give up earlier in life, turn to chocolate ice cream, milk and muffins, laser hair removal, color therapy.

One of the few approaches Coach. Even dead drunk, the guy is a magnet. And the thing is, he's not doing anything. He's just standing there alone, watching.

I have one foot out the door when he brings her over. She seems like a nice enough girl, the kind who's always saying she's sorry, who probably had braces. She smiles and it rubs off on me a little. Coach has vanished, and for a second, I think he's got coke jaw, he's out of practice, he did a lot. But no, he just went for another bump, he comes back, eyes shiny and wet.

"What do you think?" he yells in my ear.

The music is very loud, they've been turning it up as the sun rises. They sell more booze that way, I guess, people get excited.

"Nice," I say.

"So, onward?"

"To where?"

"My place? Or yours, if you'd rather."

The old dog. That's what he wanted all along. And here I was thinking I'd figured him out, that I was bringing him into my world.

The woman who used to have braces, Alicia, Belén, or something like that, turns out to be more gifted than I thought. She also takes to the coke. We end up at her place. We get on either side of her, and she grabs on to both our dicks. She closes her eyes, you can tell she likes it. I try not to think and look at the ceiling, which has glow-in-the-dark stars on it. Maybe they're her son's, he's with his dad for the weekend because Dad found a shiny new toy and now she has weekends free for "personal growth," to do things she couldn't before, because her marriage had kept her from actualizing. If the commitment she's showing now is any indication, she's one hundred percent embodying her true self.

I'm facing straight ahead, but I notice Coach keeps looking at me, my chest and then my dick, and I don't know if he likes it or if it's just curiosity. I concentrate, but I can't get hard. Braces gets tired after a while and focuses on Coach. She gets on top of him, closes her eyes, and starts to pant, he's panting too, but he doesn't close his eyes. In fact, he keeps his eyes aimed right at me while I stand up, totally flaccid, and circle the room in search of my clothes. He gestures to try and bring me back to the party.

I'm not sure if I should run out of there naked or go back over, and in the end, I go back over. Turns out I can't resist that penetrating look either. He grazes my dick, and I let him, he grabs it, I let him. At first I feel a light trembling in my testicles, as if something's about to wake up, but it evaporates.

I pull away while Alicia or Esther bobs on top of him, faster and faster, and starts to moan. If that ex knew what he was missing, he'd be sorry.

The clothes are in the living room, all mixed up. Did we undress each other? Did we kiss and touch before getting in bed? I slither into my pants, grab everything else, and get the fuck out.

The morning light is completely white, as if it's the first day on

Earth. The street smells like the drip coffee at the bars that are opening their doors, and the servers have that bitter expression you're left
with when you realize you've thrown your life away.

"There's a part of you that's lost in the cosmos. It's not your fault. These things happen. You lose your epithelial cells. Your memories dissipate. Your desires from the last seven years are floating in space. And it's killing you. All the pieces you've left behind. It's not your fault, but you have to get them back. You think it sounds crazy at first. But you can feel them coming back now: the orange semitruck you would play with when you were five, the BH bike you didn't want to share because it was shiny, and you were afraid it would get dirty. Stop there. Why were you afraid. What was going to happen to the bike. But you didn't want it to get dirty, you spent all day wondering how to maintain that shine, until you forgot. How could you have loved that bike so much and then forgotten about it? What are you not seeing? There's something important you've launched into the universe, as if it didn't belong to you. Do you see it? Focus on that."

And on and on, for a good while. Most of the group is going for it, but I can't keep my eyes shut. They're thinking about the bicycle or whatever. I can barely hold in my laughter, because they look like a bunch of idiots, the skinny blonde in horn-rimmed glasses has her face all screwed up, she's thinking of something bad, something that keeps her "suspended in the past," the times when she wanted Daddy to pay attention to her, and Daddy went off to the bar to watch the game. The big guy in the plaid shirt is red from the effort, like remembering is tougher than running a marathon. I'm dying to get out of here. Coach is looking right at me, but he's acting like he doesn't realize my eyes are open, he's smiling that smile they say we should smile for clients, but I've never been able to do it right, that's why I'm going from bad to worse.

The HR director told me it isn't punishment. The new role will help me better develop my "special skills," or so says her data. Nice try, but they "relieved" me of working with our big clients because I can't flash them a smile like that. It's a little fucked up to fraternize with these guys who, no matter how loaded they are, still complain that we're not pulling the right strings for them to leech off everyone else. If Coach didn't keep his cards so close to the chest, if he told me his trick for smiling, maybe I'd get somewhere, but with this crap about the bike, I just don't see it.

I could ask Diana for help. I slept with her, that must get me something. But now she's on the mom track, she's no fun anymore. She'll probably say something like: "You have to rise to the occasion, Carlos. Staying stuck isn't an option," and send me back to Coach.

"Carlos," Coach says when the session ends, "Carlos," and he grabs me like we're friends. "You have to let the energy flow, you're too hung up on your surroundings. You have to free yourself and encounter your cosmic being. I know you can do it. I believe in you." He shoots me that smile again, and I'm so jealous I almost hit him. He must sense it, being that he's tapped into cosmic energy and all that, and he walks off, the smile's still on his face, but he goes.

As we leave, he takes us each by the hand, very ceremonious, then shuts the door. The others stay there talking. They think it was "an amazing experience." I don't want to spoil the fun, so I take off.

Outside, the cars are rumbling. Everyone's rushing to get somewhere. That's happiness, I think, rushing to get somewhere. What bullshit. I should have just gone to the bar. It's Friday, for fuck's sake.

But really, why did I go back? It's like falling for one of those women I sometimes sleep with, the ones who act like they know you from somewhere and then you end up believing them. What a stunt. Every woman's stunt.

I'll have another. Tonight's looking good. There are two fake blondes checking me out. Why not? I've got nothing to lose. The chubby one asks if I want to dance. Her breasts bounce up and down to the rhythm of the music. *Do you believe in life after love.* This DJ knows what he's doing. Plumpy is excited, she closes her eyes and comes closer. *Maybe I'm too good for you.* That sends her over the edge. She grabs my hands and sticks them on her hips. *I don't need you anymore.* That's right, because I don't need her, I think tonight's going to be terrific.

The other one joins in. There must be a limited selection at this bar. She gets behind me. They're doing some kind of ritual. It seems like they must have practiced, like they're competing for me. Vying for my attention, putting my hands on their hips.

I start to feel warm. It's gin flooding the parts of my brain that keep "my cosmic self" out of reach. The blondes are sweating. Now that I look at them, I realize sweat is dripping down their foreheads, their upper lips shine. They're drinking whiskey, their bodies are dripping with it, bitter, sweet, intoxicating. The lights start to wear on me, on off on. That's the pulse of my dying brain, I think.

The chubby one touches my dick and takes a step back, it's not what she was hoping for. She looks discouraged. Her expression seems to say, "What rotten luck."

"Carlos, you're something else when you drink," Diana's voice, echoing in my head: "We're done, you and I. Everything is fixed now, understand?" She meant whatever her husband's deal was, which she never wanted to tell me about, whatever he did that sent her to me some Sunday mornings instead. "I'm pregnant. The IVF worked, can you believe it? Everything is fixed now, but take care of yourself, OK? You need to see someone, Carlos. This is no way to live."

And now, the blondes have gone off somewhere. Women can smell dead meat. So I grab onto the bar, and my head is burning. My head is on fire.

"What's wrong with you. You *lose* heat through your head," Angélica would say. So serious, with that doctorly look on her face. And me: intimidated. Like a bug. No, Angélica, not me, I don't lose heat through my head. She knew all about mutations, genetic combinations, but when it came to me, she knew nothing, just like the others. Every woman's stunt.

"You're the kind of guy who does things just to do them," she told me one day. And me, I was happy. Because that meant she liked me. But no, it didn't mean anything. It was, what was it? An objective observation?

It was because I could get it up without thinking.

"This relationship is defective," I told her.

"Yes," she said, satisfied, nearly suicidal. "Isn't it fantastic that we know that already?"

She takes my hand and places it on her breast. It's small, like a tangerine. There's no going back.

It's the skinny blonde in the horn-rimmed glasses. I would have gone for the brunette, but she disappeared.

It all happened during the last session of the week, when I confessed. She turned to me immediately and said, "I don't care about that." And she meant it. Lying is not allowed. Insults, yes; punching walls, sure; not being on speaking terms with your family, OK. But not lying.

At first, I thought that rule seemed absurd. Like getting rid of the clothes you don't like, or telling yourself every morning, a hundred times, it doesn't matter what people think. But then I started to catch on. It's like Coach and his hideous mustache. It hasn't stopped being hideous, we've just accepted it.

"You all must think I look pretty average for someone who works with beings in transit."

We had to say yes, there was no other option.

"Well, it's true," he said. "That's part of my SES, my 'solidified external self.' There's very little I can do to change it."

"You could shave," I said.

"Thanks for your contribution, Carlos. I always appreciate your candor. Yes, of course, that's something I could do, but if I were to do that, there would be other things to worry about—my teeth, my greasy hair. I'm sure you've all noticed my hair can be a bit greasy? But that hasn't kept you from coming back, has it? Because the SES is only outward appearance, and all of you, when you took that first step, when you came here that first time, showed you were able to overcome it. Now, I want each of you to give the group an update on your SES."

That's when I told them I couldn't get it up. It was the best thing that happened all day. Then some people went on and on about their weight, their height, their teeth, but nothing really genuine, not like what I had shared, I really do have a good SES. That's when the others figured out I speak from the heart, I'm the real deal, and that's why Malena, the skinny blonde, responded so well. Or that's the theory.

"If you think about it, it's a miracle," Malena says while she moves my hand to her genitals.

Right away, she gets wet. She has no trouble getting turned on, her legs close and she starts to moan, gently at first and then faster. She tells me to go harder, rub her clit, grab her ass with my other hand. There was a time when I would have gone crazy for that. Now, nothing. But she doesn't seem to mind. She says she's over penetration.

She's so thin it sometimes makes me feel sick, but there's something

I like about her, maybe her eyes, pale enough so when she looks at you, you're not sure if she's looking at you, or looking through you at something else. I'm not crazy about her, but she won't let me out of her sight.

"That's good," she says. "You don't have to like me like that."

She pours tea into the cups she set out on the coffee table. The house is full of little Buddha statues and incense burners. Instead of sofas, there are a couple long, thin purple cushions on the floor. She has on a dragon-print satin robe, and her hair is down, shoulder length.

There's something inside me that wants to scream and break things. She seems to understand. "It's OK if you want to go now, I won't be upset." But instead of going, I lean back on a cushion and light a cigarette.

Lisa, the brunette, has fully stopped showing up, but no one has asked any questions. We're all free to follow our SES. I've been watching Coach to see if I can figure anything out. Maybe he seemed down for a while, eyes duller than before, but he's completely over it now. I tell myself I need to stay in my SES, but my curiosity gets to me. I ask Malena, "Whatever happened to Lisa?"

"I'm not sure."

She doesn't want to tell me. In the sessions, Malena has no problem spilling her secrets, but she doesn't like to talk about other people. I try looking at her like I'm dying to know, and surprise, surprise, she gives in. Maybe I'm catching on.

"She's involved with someone at work, a woman. That's what's kept her from coming back."

"Because it's a woman?"

She looks at me. If she knew about Coach and Lisa, I'm sure she wouldn't tell me, but I don't think she does. She's one of those people who doesn't realize what's happening right in front of them.

"No. Why would that be a problem? That's ridiculous. You know it wouldn't matter even if she had three husbands. That stuff isn't important."

"So what is important?"

"You already know that, the SES and the cosmic being."

I laugh. "No, important to you, Malena. What's important to *you*?"

She gives me that transparent look. Maybe she's going to cry.

"The development of the SES. I just told you that."

"OK."

I try bringing my sarcasm down a notch. The last thing I want is to make anybody cry.

"Then why is it a problem that she's with a woman? Why can't she keep working on her SES?"

"Because the woman she works with is a bad influence. Lisa says she doesn't believe in sincerity."

Aha. We're getting somewhere now. I nod so she'll go on, I want to hear what comes next. I'm enjoying the process so much I might even be getting hard.

"She told me in the bathroom, when we were changing. She said she was 'sick of all this sincerity crap,' those were her exact words, and that's when I realized. It's because of the woman, the other scientist."

"What kind of scientists are they? Researchers?"

"No, they work at a big fertility clinic. The Plant, I think it's called. But that's beside the point. The point is, this other woman wanted to drive her away from her cosmic being. She saw it as a threat. This stuff happens all the time. You're still new," she says, running her fingers through my hair. "You'll understand soon."

I can't speak, I might pass out, this is just what I needed. What if Angélica is Lisa's lover? That sounds just like her, I swear. Sincerity's overrated. What if my ex is a lesbian and all that baggage she thought was mine was actually hers?

Malena thinks I'm interested in her reflections. "The point is, the woman wants to keep her stuck. She doesn't want any competition, because she's not ready to handle it."

I can feel the tears coming when Malena gets on top of me and her robe falls open. She understood everything backwards, she thinks I liked Lisa. She puts my hands on her orange-like breasts, and I let her. She doesn't touch my dick, she just wants me to touch her.

The contact with her skin puts me in a kind of vivid dream. She starts moaning again, showing me where to touch her and how, and I have a revelation: this must be what I have to do, touch Malena until she can't handle the pleasure, and I can't handle the pain. All my pain goes toward her smooth yellow body in little waves, and she accepts it and doesn't critique it. And I see that it's working, I'll have to tell Coach about this, he's a good guy, I'm realizing now, what's really bad is lying: when you tell the truth, things go well. I think I'm ascending in my SES.

María

We swim slower and slower.

As our bellies grow, our lung capacities shrink. Still, this is the best form of exercise for mothers and fetuses.

Jacob, the water aerobics instructor, doesn't let us take breaks. He tells us this is his calling. To make sure these babies are born with strong hearts.

According to the rankings of gyms and prenatal exercise classes, Jacob is the most trustworthy, best-qualified instructor. Trustworthiness is subjective, but when the sample size is large enough, it can be represented in a very accurate way.

Jacob has more than a thousand ratings, so I trust the results are sound.

While I swim, I entertain myself by thinking about things like this. I miss my job. Manuela is determined to keep me out of the office and mostly resting until after the child is born, and what they're having me do remotely isn't enough.

Any junior employee could cross-validate models in her sleep. But

Manuela has reminded me that stress is a major risk-factor during pregnancy, and the data supports that. I've always listened to her before, and she hasn't once led me astray.

I've scored well on physical fitness tests.

So there's no reason not to take her advice. Also, although I'm approaching my eighth month of what's basically leave, I'm still getting my regular paycheck. In that respect, I can't complain.

But I'm bored. The afternoons are the worst. At first, I would take lots of walks, the second most beneficial activity for pregnant individuals. But I don't do that anymore, because it's fall now, and it never stops raining, and my belly is heavy, it weighs me down, and my thighs ache, too, so walking is uncomfortable. Those of us with reduced mobility are lucky to have the internet.

Dad hasn't stopped insisting on moving in with me. At least for a few months, he says. I remind him that if he moves, no one will be keeping an eye on the shop. He has a terrible assistant, the son of a neighbor who's out of work, completely unequipped. I know this because as kids we were classmates, then they held him back because he couldn't add two and two.

Anyway, I hope he decides not to come. It's very possible he will, that's how much he lets his emotions control him. I'm lucky I'm more like Mom, someone has to keep a cool head, and especially now, since there will be three of us.

It's a girl.

When they told me, I thought: I'd rather have a boy.

But I made the sweetest face possible, which I've been practicing all along, paying attention to other moms. Mastering that was much harder for me than the weight gain, the body aches, the morning sickness. At least when you're nauseous you know what's coming.

I don't know why I imagined a boy. Because a higher percentage of scientists are male, probably.

I couldn't stop thinking about it for days. What if I can't relate to her? If she's obsessed with boys and it makes her crazy? I've seen that happen with some of my friends' kids. Or what if she's really cutesy and wants to wear princess clothes all the time? Just imagining that made me sweat, like I used to before the pregnancy.

But then it passed. Whatever she's like, she'll be mine, and that's what counts.

Sometimes the water aerobics instructor will say things like, "Folks, the child you're carrying right now is yours, more yours than anything else in this life. Remember that."

On those occasions, we say nothing. For long enough to remind him he's just our water aerobics instructor, and no one has asked for his thoughts on our situation. But he doesn't take the hint. Excessive physical activity can sometimes have consequences for the mind, and judging by his muscles, he's almost certainly overdone it.

Later on, inevitably, the phrases that small-time cheerleader shouts come back to you.

Class is already ending, and I'm relieved. It's harder and harder to get through the forty-five minutes.

A little underwater swimming now, I think. I like to finish up with that, even if just for a minute or two. The instructor says it's not advisable after seven months, but he has no idea how it feels to suddenly lose all that extra weight, like becoming yourself again.

So I push off and kick to the middle, hoping no one sees, and I have the urge to try and make it across without coming up for air. A second later, I see another future mother coming toward me, swimming the opposite way. I don't recognize her.

I shift to the right a little so we both have plenty of room. We make eye contact as we pass each other. There's a look on her face I interpret as surprise. But that doesn't make any sense.

I can't stop thinking about the other future mother's facial expression, and by the time I get home, I've realized I got it wrong. It wasn't surprise, it was panic.

I want to be sure, so I click through pages and pages of facial expressions, and yes, there's no doubt in my mind, the look on her face was fear, textbook fear.

I can barely sleep, tossing and turning, trying to find a comfortable position, but it's impossible. I get up, put on my goggles, open my eyes wide, and look in the mirror.

Angélica • Diana • María

I decided to stop looking at Hester's notebook when I saw the photos of the two babies. They looked so much alike that when we hung them up in the waiting room, we confused Diana's daughter, Moe, with María's, Ariadna.

From that moment on, things went completely haywire.

Lisa showed up one day and told me that she was finding her true self at whatever therapy she'd been going to for a year now.

Then she confessed she'd been messing around with her guru. Of course, I thought, soon she'll find out he sleeps with all the women he works with, he'll break her heart. But no. It was Lisa who ended things with him, and ended the therapy, too. That happened the night we had sex for the first time.

Her body is springy and aromatic, as if it's made of moss.

A few days ago she went down for croissants for breakfast, and I found her journal in a drawer in her room. In the entry after our first night together, she wrote:

"I like how she looks at my breasts, almost scientific, comparing them to hers. I like when she makes me coffee, black, and tells me that I'm perfect, she doesn't want me to gain an ounce. I like when she brushes my hair. I like being her doll, when she talks to me about math, that she ruminates on the origins of the universe. I like that she gets breakfast right, that she feeds me. I like that animal mercy."

I was moved. Suddenly Lisa was everything I'd been waiting for.

I wanted to keep reading, even though I knew it was wrong, or because I knew it was wrong—I've lost all sense of why I do what I do. But Lisa was quick, and I was only able to glance at the latest entry: "Fall in love, stop thinking so much, detecting genetic mutations."

This morning she told me she wanted to talk.

"I'm in love," she said, beaming. "Don't ask me how."

I was about to say I was too, that she was the only thing that made sense, when she added, "It's a guy I met in therapy."

"I thought you stopped going," I managed to say while she went over to the coffee maker and poured herself a cup.

"I'm not, but I still meet up with some of them sometimes. You're going to love him. You'll see. He's perfect for me. Want breakfast?"

She kept talking, saying she'd finally found herself, she finally knew who she was, she was serious about him. I could barely stay in my chair. I held tight to my coffee mug and tried to take a sip, but just the smell of it made me gag.

So there is no law of causality. Things happen because they do. There's no action and reaction, no cause and effect. The whole universe is a huge chaotic mass in which the only rule is, save yourself if you can.

Save yourself now, in this meaningless second. Salvation is now or never.

But my old ways get the better of me, I can't fully accept the state of things, so I look for something to grab at, however minor. I reopen Hester's notebook and start a new section: "Unknown events."

My first entry is:

"Strange resemblance between the only successes in the last six months. Possible causes: a) degeneration of gametes, b) contamination in the lab, c) genetic modification designed in the lab? d) unknown."

DECLINE

Diana • María

I'm tired of things only half working. Take Telefónica, for example. If they get the idea that we're breaking our contract, they'll shut off our data, or they'll charge us for a service that should be included, never mind that we pay our bill in full month after month. Sure, you can make a complaint and maybe they'll do something, but that takes too long, and it's exhausting. When things only half work, it's exhausting.

Blasco still files complaints. Ever since Moe was born, he's been very particular. Latoya says she doesn't know why I worry so much. When I tell her he spends hours organizing closets or cataloging CDs he doesn't listen to anymore she insists it's all very normal. That's what happens with Blasco, everyone takes his side. I could hardly believe their reaction, or nonreaction, when he finally opened up about his addiction to what was essentially child pornography. They responded like it was nothing, like he had jaywalked, maybe, or run a red light.

According to Latoya, the problem is I expect too much. I see Blasco as half a husband, and Moe, I hate to say it, I really hate to say it, but Moe is like half a daughter. To Latoya, though, my husband and daughter are perfect. "You have it all," she says constantly.

I try to explain that Blasco isn't the way he used to be, that he barely registers anything, and that Moe is completely oblivious, too, no matter what I do for her, but Latoya simply repeats another one of her favorites, "We all have our flaws." That's what she's like now, after chemo. Tolerant to the extreme. It's not that I don't see the value in her position. In fact, she's the only person I can talk to about Carlos, and it's because I know she won't judge me, she says that's normal too. But sometimes all her indifference starts to get under my skin, and I feel like grabbing her shoulders and shaking her, yelling at her to wake up.

Moe turned eleven today, and I decided I've had it. I'm determined to solve our problems, because if I don't do it, who will. Maybe it's the rain that brought all this on. It's your typical November downpour, just like the day Moe was born. That afternoon, in that green-and-white hospital room, the water was hitting the windows so hard there was a moment when I thought if Moe didn't hurry, a flood would finish us off.

Or maybe it's not the rain. Maybe it's that I first noticed all this, the half-working of things, many months ago. Sometimes I look at myself, and at Moe, and at Blasco, and each of us seems divided, literally split in two, as if someone had drawn lines right down our middles. And one of the halves, typically the left one, is disappearing.

For the last eleven years, I've done nothing but try to get things functioning properly, fully. It doesn't matter what I do, I can't seem to pull it off. The trip to the Caribbean, which I planned by myself for Blasco and me when Moe was barely two, did absolutely nothing to get him out of his slump. I took care of everything, flights, hotels, guided tours, someone to watch Moe. I even made sure to use all the best data to pick out restaurants ahead of time.

When we got there, I felt something stirring between us, like desire being reborn, but no, it was just an illusion. We were the same as we'd been before. He was off in his own little world, and I couldn't let go of the feeling that something was missing, as if someone had cut out a part of our bodies, a vital, invisible organ.

Then I bought the new house in Zone 4, with the hundred-square-foot living room and one full bathroom for each of us. But that didn't do it either. Blasco is now unmoved as a rule, and Moe—basically his double, biological or not—is following in his footsteps. She's reaching the age where they only care about socializing and pop songs, which she constantly sings to herself, even when she's eating. I've told her a thousand times that it's disgusting and unhygienic, that it makes me want to throw up, but she couldn't care less. Naturally, Blasco doesn't flinch. When it comes to manners, I'm basically single parenting.

So nothing is as it should be, and no matter how hard I try, nothing's enough. But that's all going to change. A few weeks ago, I heard about a woman, María Lebrel—working on the key accounts has its perks. She's a healer, and she gives talks at her house in the mountains. From what I've heard, it's no exaggeration to say she works miracles.

She has no website, almost no digital footprint. She's like a ghost. All I could find in our digital archive were some articles from a decade ago. Apparently, before she went off to the countryside, she was a famous big data analyst, but she chose to change her life radically and became a spiritual guide. There's not much information about her approach, but what do we have to lose?

The meetings are family-friendly, so Moe comes along. She's at that age where you're not sure if it's OK to leave them alone.

Though María lives an hour outside the city, the meeting is packed. We almost don't fit in the dining room. There are about thirty of us, not counting the children, who are playing in the yard. Really, it's not a yard, it's more of a terrace, with a granite slab in the middle and reddish vines climbing up the nearby walls. There's also a swing rigged up with rope and a leather saddle, hanging from the only tree on the property. It's all very charming and rustic, it has a certain air of neglect.

The inside isn't in much better shape. There's a huge old rug on the living-room floor that could probably use a shampooing, mismatched chairs of different sizes, a few leather poufs, and a space heater.

There are no empty chairs, so we sit on some big cushions, the kind that were popular in offices in the nineties. My nose hasn't stopped tingling, so I'd guess there's plenty of dust, and I start to get nervous just thinking about what might happen with all the germs and bacteria. Everyone else seems calm but expectant. Most of them appear to have been here several times. They're all speaking in hushed tones, like they're trying to be unobtrusive, or like when a play is about to start.

María seems to be in no rush, so we strike up a conversation. Or more accurately, I talk, and Blasco, as usual, doesn't open his mouth. There are a lot of married couples still in their work clothes, like us. There are also some people who showed up alone, most of them women.

"I wish she would come out. I was here for the first time last month, and I think about what she told us every day," one of them says.

"Is it just one session a month?" asks another.

The first woman nods. "It's all part of her philosophy. We have to do the work, she can't do it for us. We can't come all the way out here every day."

The excitement is palpable in the room. We're all waiting for something to happen. It's been a long time since I was present for something like this, maybe since the company's first few board meetings. The current of energy fills me with hope, I feel my heart pounding in my chest. It reminds me of when they put me in charge of investments and I knew exactly what to do to make us more profitable than ever.

María finally comes out. She looks normal as can be: average height, hair pulled into a tight ponytail, wearing a loose-fitting knit dress that hides some extra weight. I have the feeling I've seen her before, but I couldn't say where. She hasn't put makeup on, which makes her look old or wise.

She sits on the ground in front of us. The room holds its breath, she crosses her legs and smiles.

"I've been where you are right now," she says.

She pauses for a second, then, "I've been crushed, brought right down to freezing, I couldn't move a muscle, my heart stopped pumping blood."

Another pause.

"Let me tell you a story. A few years ago, my whole body was in pain, my mind was in pain. But that wasn't the worst part. The worst part was, I thought I was happy. I had a good job, I was making more than I could spend. I bought designer clothes, I routinely paid more for one piece of furniture than I paid for everything in this house. I lived in Zone 6."

There's a murmur in the room. I'd guess that many of the attendees also live in Zone 6. Compared to them, Blasco and I are destitute.

"I had a beautiful apartment all to myself, I'd worked my ass off. Don't tell me that's not enough. My intellect, which I always considered my greatest gift, had driven me there—my intellect alone. I felt good, I felt better than good. I felt invincible.

"In the mornings, a driver picked me up and took me to work. The company didn't want us distracted with things like driving or parking. They wanted us fresh and alert, performing at one hundred. And that's what we did, we performed at one hundred percent.

"During my time in the glass tower, I made calculations to help improve people's lives. We worked out what makes us happy: shopping or nightlife, spending on clothes or leisure, travel or gifts.

"At night I went home and put into practice whatever we'd learned. I bought a hot air balloon ride, I bought weekend trips in cities across Europe. Also clothing and household goods. Because buying material objects is less satisfactory in the long run, but it's very satisfactory short-term, and it was important, when you were buying, to take both timeframes into account. I even bought a cruise, which I went on with my father—buying things for others seemed to increase happiness too.

"Everything was going according to plan. I had money, success, good friends, and a great boss, Manuela."

The silence in the room reaches its peak.

María takes a sip of water from the glass someone put in front of her. She breathes and changes postures, from sukhasana to vajrasana.

"Manuela was my guide. Although I'd never been in the same room as her, I trusted her like my own mother. More than I trusted my mother. My mother had raised us, and she had worked in a few department stores, but she wasn't especially worldly. Manuela was. She traveled, she ran a huge company, and, most importantly, she treated us like her own children.

"But something happened. Something always happens, right?"

We all nod, Blasco tries to stay still though he must be uncomfortable, and I notice a prickling in my stomach and chest, like something is waking up.

"From one day to the next, everything fell apart. I couldn't sleep, I found food revolting, I had questions, uncomfortable questions. They didn't seem so uncomfortable then, of course, just critical to our research: In our attempts to define happiness, weren't we leaving out certain variables? Sure, it was all fine and good to buy an experience, but an experience is more satisfying if you share it with someone else, and what's the ideal profile for that person, and how should you find them?

"It was enough to derail everything. Manuela must have known. Did she tell me? No. Instead, she said she wanted to find me 'a way out.' The company had paid for our eggs to be frozen a while back, so everything seemed, suddenly, very simple. I did IVF and had Ariadna.

"Easy, right? I stop thinking so much, I go back to work, problem solved. That's what I believed was going to happen, while I was pregnant. Manuela would email me every month, checking in, sending encouragement.

"What more could you want. I'm missing work, and my boss isn't even annoyed. She genuinely supports me. She cares about my well-being.

"At that point, I really wasn't working anymore. At first I didn't realize, with all the excitement, the physical changes, the preparations. But around my third trimester, I started to feel like something was off. New humans always bring clarity, don't they?

"In my eighth month, I was sure of it. Why would they give an employee in perfect health nine months of leave?

"I checked every database, my company password still worked. It was quite common for pregnant women to experience paranoia, especially in the third trimester.

"OK, that explained it.

"But I couldn't shake the feeling that something was wrong, so I decided to write to Manuela. I told her what I wanted: for them to bring me back on full-time as soon as I'd given birth. I was doing great, and the company had done enough for me. They'd been losing time and money, and I'd been losing time.

"She was very polite, as always. She told me it was no problem for the company, that they cared a great deal about my health, things like that. Like I told you, she was the perfect boss. But Manuela made one mistake. Or, not a mistake, it was the only thing she could do. She used her usual sign-off: 'Hugs and kisses.'

"To which you'll say: how lovely, she's so sweet. And that's what I always thought, too, ever since she replaced the old CEO—a man with a big mustache who nobody trusted with anything, not even weekend plans or favorite desserts—and started leading research and development.

"'Hugs and kisses?' I thought. That's strange. I'm about to have a baby. Wouldn't it have made more sense to say 'hoping all goes smoothly,' or 'send photos as soon as you can'? Something wasn't adding up, but what. I mean, Manuela had always signed off that way, 'hugs and kisses' was her trademark.

"I started going through all the emails she'd sent us. My due date was swiftly approaching, Ariadna was ready to come out, and there

I was, up all night, thinking about Manuela. Then I remembered the minimum recommended amount of sleep for a pregnant person, and I felt awful. I tried to fit in naps in the mornings and afternoons. With a very full stomach.

"The worst thing you can do if you're about to go into labor."

Laughter in the room.

"And then one day I was tossing and turning, suffering through the worst heartburn of my life, and that's when I realized. Manuela didn't exist. Manuela was a machine, an AI programmed to keep us all working at 'optimal levels,' and, if necessary, 'arrange for our departures.' Because that's what they were doing—arranging for my departure.

"The thing is, when you're in that field, and that high up, you know how to poke around. You can hack into almost anything if you're motivated enough, and I was motivated enough. So I hacked into our system and got my proof.

"There was no mistaking it. For the last two years, I'd been talking to a machine. I had trusted a machine. I had thought of a machine as my own mother.

"And then I regurgitated all the food I had eaten that week."

More laughter.

"After that came the panic attack. Something was broken on a global scale, that's for sure. But something was also broken inside of me, really, terribly broken.

"And, as often happens in situations like these, I went into labor."

Laughter erupts in the room, increasing in volume. María breaks out of her posture and looks at her audience. You can tell she's pleased by the laughter, but not too much.

"Now I want you to go home and think about all this. Think, and act accordingly. Don't come back if you find your way out of the labyrinth. I'll be happy for you. Or come back, if you feel you should."

When she's finished with her talk, María leaves. Without approaching anyone, without another word.

At the next session, María keeps us waiting for more than an hour. I'm very annoyed at first—I hate it when people are late—but then we start talking with some of the others, and it passes. Some of these people are actually very interesting. I'm especially intrigued by a woman in her mid-fifties who says she's an artist. Her name is Momo and she makes performances. Blasco, who seems to be in a good mood today, asks her what kind of performances, and she chews her lip a little and says it depends, one day she takes frozen entrails out of a box, lies down, and arranges them over her torso, other days she does nothing, just looks at the audience, or doesn't look, or sits with her back turned and breathes. It's all very free form, she says.

Momo's the kind of woman you can't help but notice. She's taller than average, maybe just shy of six feet, and her hair is short and white—I think it's her natural color. As soon as she turns around, I can tell she's much closer than we are to finding her way, as María puts it, out of the labyrinth. Meanwhile I've made no progress, though for weeks I've thought of nothing else.

I'm meditating on that when María appears and sits down without a word. She starts right in with a question, "So, what did you make of the story I shared last session?"

Momo rises to the occasion: "The AI represents your hidden desires, your nightmares. You didn't want to face them, but you did it anyway, and that's when your true growth began."

María looks at Momo, it's possible there's slight approval in her eyes, but she says nothing. Momo seems disappointed. She tries to hide it, though, straightening on her ottoman and giving half a smile.

After that reception, no one seems willing to speak.

María insists. "Please, participate. It's important we get a sense of where we are, as a group. The time is now. If you'd like, if it would make things easier, feel free to raise your hands."

Moe is with Ariadna, María's daughter. They're sitting at a table that was probably used for al fresco dining, in better times. Now it's full of junk, much like the surrounding terrace. A tray for food, some coffee cups, something that looks like a sewing box but could also contain a puzzle or toy, it's hard to tell at this distance. All the clutter makes me anxious. I couldn't live that way.

I try to let the thought go, because during these last few weeks of mindfulness, I've realized those are the kinds of thoughts keeping me trapped in the labyrinth. My mindset needs to change now, I can't keep putting it off.

I watch the girls a second longer while the silence stretches on. Moe holds out her palm, and Adriadna takes it and runs her index finger along it, maybe tracing its lines. When she's done, she puts her own hand face-up on the table so Moe can inspect it.

Then an impulse takes hold of me, and without knowing what

I'm about to say, I start talking. "What matters, I think, is making decisions. We can't just sit here paralyzed while life steamrolls us."

María looks at me, she reaches toward me with both hands. You can feel the tension in the room. Blasco looks at me, too, shocked, though he tries to hide it. I've been begging him to support me in this, to join me here.

"That's right," María says, coming toward me and grabbing my hands. Her touch is cool, almost liquid. "That's right."

María goes back to her place in the middle of the circle, the corners of her mouth slightly upturned. Although I wouldn't call her beautiful, she now looks much more attractive, as if her own personal light has gone on. When she got close, I noticed her scent. I'm sure she doesn't wear perfume, she smells like wet earth. There was a time when I would have found that off-putting, but now it's having a calming effect—maybe my breakthrough is coming.

"You've moved me, Diana."

The attendees exhale collectively, as if they've been holding their breath. There are tears on more than one face. Some people hug. I look at them and stay quiet, unsure if there's something I should be doing. But then María gives us all a peaceful, authentic smile and leaves the room.

When my heartrate finally lowers—it was high, like I'd just run a hundred meters—I realize I have more energy than ever. I feel so full of life I even offer to drive us home. I get behind the steering wheel, we head back. Blasco doesn't say much, just sneaks an occasional look at me. I know those looks well, he's afraid I'll lose control on a curve. Normally that would annoy me, but today it doesn't affect me at all.

"Wasn't that amazing? It's like she's helping us access another universe. Another plane of reality. I can't wait for next month," I say once we've reached the main road.

Moe is in the back seat, unconcerned with our conversation, looking at a drawing Ariadna did of her.

"Yeah, really fantastic," Blasco says, in a tone that could be either sincere or sarcastic, which everyone in the world seems to find funny except for me.

A week later, I get a letter from María. It has to be the first time we've received physical mail in years:

"Diana, you've made an impression on me. You're one of a few students who I believe have a real capacity for transformation. I'd like you to join me on Fridays for weekly private sessions. Bring Moe. She and Ariadna seem to get along well."

Reading it I feel excited, like I do when I pass a competency test for a promotion. *I knew it, I knew it*, I think—finally, things are going to be different, the way they should have been all along. I hug Moe, who is, as usual, playing on her phone, and her body seems more solid. She winces, she's not used to me hugging her anymore, but she lets me for a second, then she turns around and says, "Mom!"

In that voice she uses to tell me she wants me to leave her alone but also that she didn't entirely hate the show of affection.

Then she slips off to her room, trotting on those long legs, which she didn't get from me, and for the first time in a very long time, I don't get the feeling that part of her is fading.

The road to María's village is narrow, a little steep. It's not terribly dangerous, but I still prefer Blasco to drive. There are oaks on either side, increasingly dense as we ascend, and their leaves, already yellow, have formed a carpet in shades of ochre, a picture of autumn. Our journey through the trees feels like our first step on the path toward a fuller life. I roll down the window and breathe in the aroma of damp and decay. Blasco looks surprised, because normally I keep the windows up and the AC on, to avoid allergens and insects.

I'll admit that when Moe was born, something similar happened. A kind of internal silence took hold, the feeling that we were complete. Then she grew up, obviously, and the feeling disappeared. But this time it's different, I can sense it in every cell.

Blasco parks and goes to walk around the village, and I enter the house.

The girls, who seem naturally on the same wavelength, go out to play on the swing. Scattered here and there are red leaves from the vine that crowds the walls of the house, which, now that I look at it, is a kind of climbing plant I've never seen.

The session is intense but very effective. I understand, though María doesn't say so explicitly, that we need to commit to a new way of living, one that involves greater awareness, another level of awareness.

I get working on that right away on Saturday. The first thing I do is go through the house and put anything we don't use anymore, anything that's anchoring us to our previous, false way of life, in boxes. There are four kinds of boxes: things we don't use, things we've never used, things we're never going to use, things we have no reason to use.

It's hardest for me to part with the maternity swimsuit I only used once. Jacob, the instructor, had excellent ratings, but when I got in with the rest of the pregnant women, I couldn't stop thinking about how the water was probably teeming with germs, and I almost fled. I promised myself that once Moe was born I would squeeze back into my swimsuit and conquer my fear of contamination once and for all, but I never did. Once I've tossed the maternity suit in a box, the rest follows easily.

I have no problem getting rid of Moe's tiny baptism outfit. It's more challenging to throw out the perfume I've been wearing for fifteen years. I looked everywhere for a fragrance that felt right for me. Most of the ones you see at department stores are excessive, or make me sneeze. I had to contact a place in London that makes custom scents based on a person's answers to survey questions. Before putting it in a box, I open it one last time, breathe in the base notes, vanilla and mandarin, and then there's that hint of something metallic, which I've never known how to describe but which gives it that spark, a touch of danger. "It's over," I say. That's the smell of the past. The last thing I get rid of is the *World Encyclopedia of Entrepreneurship*, which I bought when I was thinking about starting my own consulting firm.

On Sunday, I have so much energy that, to celebrate, and to say goodbye to our old lives and the things we have no need for, I take Blasco and Moe out to the pizzeria on our street.

The pizza is good, as usual. I get a marinara, and Moe gets barbecued chicken. I wouldn't normally let her order that garbage, but we're celebrating, I turn a blind eye.

Moe eats, smacking her lips, and tells us that in her science class, she had to dissect a rat. "It was disgusting," she says.

But she has that gleam in her eye, as if she's just discovered something. It makes me happy to see her like that. At least she has my adventurous spirit. "It was all gooey inside," she explains. "And it had everything, just tiny, a heart, lungs, a stomach . . . with food inside."

When she gets to that part, she pauses, it seems she was fascinated by the contents of the rat's stomach, there was something that looked like corn, or maybe like popcorn kernels.

"Another girl took it all out."

"Not you?" Blasco asks, enjoying the story.

"No way."

Moe finishes eating her pizza and orders white-chocolate pudding—something else that would normally be off-limits.

The next Friday, we go back to María's village. Blasco turns on the radio, he likes listening to the news while he drives, and although we sometimes argue because I like to drive in silence, today I let him. The big story is, once again, the Transnational Regional Bloc. Two experts are discussing possible routes for implementation, "strong leadership will obviously be vital," they say. They also seem to agree it would improve things overall, strengthening local economies and reducing the gap between rich and poor countries. Together we'll get out of this "extraordinary situation," they conclude.

"Bah," Blasco puffs. "We're in trouble. They have no sense of reality. Did you notice no one says 'crisis' now? Even though, economically speaking, everything's pointing straight at one, and has been for so long the word has completely lost its effect."

That's not exactly true, and Blasco knows it. What we're experiencing is, in actuality, the economic system adapting to new circumstances. If he cared to read the reports we put out every quarter, he'd understand.

"Remember when they were calling it an 'adjustment period'?" he continues. "Then a 'recovery cycle,' then a 'short-term imbalance.' Now all you hear is 'extraordinary situation,' doesn't matter if it's local news or international, it's always that same exact phrase, 'situation extraordinaire,' 'situazione straordinaria," 'situaçao extraordinaria,' and those are just the ones I understand, I'd bet money it's the same in all the others."

Blasco exhales, ponders a moment, then adds, "All they do is say over and over, 'extraordinary times call for extraordinary measures,' 'humanity is facing a great challenge,' and 'all of us need to wake up and start doing our part.' Have you noticed that?"

I look at him, not sure what to say. He's convinced he has an excellent understanding of geopolitics, and for years, he's had a taste for the apocalypse, as if he alone knows what's coming. The truth is, I'd like it if Blasco took his own mindset into account, if he stopped and considered the fact that he's causing problems, too, but everything in its time. Right now, I'd settle for him calming down, so I just nod and say, "You're right, things are really bad."

It's not the response he was hoping for, but he seems satisfied enough. When we arrive, he volunteers to keep an eye on the girls while they play. From a distance, the children look surprisingly alike.

María is cool and collected, as always. We sit on the couch and she offers me tea. It's bitter, something I'm never had before. I don't really like it, but I don't tell her. It must have its curative properties.

I find the first few minutes puzzling: María asks me about Moe, what she likes, what apps she uses, what subscriptions she has. How she does in school. It starts to feel like we're just two moms chatting in the school pickup line, and it's not that it bothers me, exactly, but it's certainly not what I'm paying for, and the one-on-one sessions aren't cheap.

When we've gone on that way for a while, exchanging trivial information about the girls' favorite movies or hairstyles, she suddenly stops midsentence, looks me dead in the eye, and grabs my hands. "Diana," she says, "You need to find what's poisoning you. Find it, and destroy it." She lets go of my hands the next second and returns to the conversation like nothing has happened. She says something about hair dyes, how none of them are natural even when the packaging claims they are. I'm not able to follow the thread, her advice has thrown me off balance. I don't know if I should look in her eyes and respond, or follow her lead and carry on normally.

She doesn't seem too worried about my reaction and proposes we go out back. I follow her, moved, feeling that something quite significant has just happened, though I'm not exactly sure what.

On Sunday we go to the group session. I haven't stopped thinking about what María said since Friday, but I haven't unlocked it yet. I'm a little nervous she'll call on me, ask me directly, but she's focused on her talk, and if she's thinking of me at all, she doesn't let on.

"I'd like to share some reflections with you," she says. "This month has been very intense for Ariadna and me."

When she talks about herself, she always includes Ariadna, like they're a unit.

"One of you has crossed over a threshold," she continues. "That doesn't happen every day."

She doesn't say my name, but I know she's referring to me, and a trembling starts in my belly.

"What happens when we cross?" María goes on. "Well, it's hard to say, because each of you will have a different experience. I can't tell you what it means for your fellow journeyer, either—they're still on the way. But I can tell you about what happened when I transcended for the first time, because that movement has already been completed. Bear with me, please, as I said, I'm a little emotional. When this happens, there's no turning back, and anyone in proximity to the person who's transcending will learn things, for better or worse."

She glances toward me.

"My first transcendence happened around the time Ariadna was born, when I realized my only stable relationship was with a computer." We all laugh.

"Ariadna wouldn't stop crying, I was starving all the time, my friend, the AI, had fired me via email, and in the middle of all that, my dad had the nerve to die." We laughed again, but just a little, because it seemed like too much to laugh at a father's death.

"So my only friend had betrayed me, and I had no idea what to do next. Well, I knew I needed to bury my dad. Corpses don't have much patience with that kind of thing."

We laugh again, this time with greater confidence.

"We cremated him. You try burying your father while you're breastfeeding a ten-day-old. They told me it was the most efficient option. I checked the data, I still had access, and they were right.

"Two weeks later, the nightmares started: my father returned from the grave to remind me I hadn't buried him, which had been his wish. He shook me by the shoulders and told me that as punishment he was taking me with him somewhere else, because I had been a bad daughter, and I was being a bad mom.

"I looked for concise definitions of 'bad daughter' and 'bad mom,' but the data was inconclusive. I don't remember how long things went on that way—maybe a few weeks. Until one night when Dad showed up in my dream again, and told me again I'd deprived him of his burial, that he was turning in his little slot in the wall at the cemetery, he was cursing me, and I decided to talk to him. Up until that moment, I always stayed quiet, I listened to what the man had to say, which was quite a lot.

"'OK, that's enough,' I told him. 'I've had it up to here. Not only did you go and die right when I needed you most, now you're coming back just to make my life harder. If that's all you're going to do, I forbid you from appearing. If you're going to show up, you have to help me with Ariadna, otherwise, stay put, and anyway, isn't Mom there? Wouldn't you rather be with her? Or are you driving her crazy too?'

"My father looked at me, he'd gone pale. Well, he'd been pale for a while, keep in mind he was dead."

We broke into laughter.

"Then he shook his head, as if to say I was hopeless, and disappeared. And that was the last time he ever bothered me. Now he's just around, when I dream about family or memories, always with my mother, always on his best behavior—the good kind of dead."

María stops talking. It's not clear if she's done or just pausing. We stay silent. Some couples look at each other, others nod.

"What did I learn from that transcendence? Well, you can look at it lots of ways. My interpretation was: from now on, no man, dead or alive, is going to fuck up my life. Come to think of it, no machine either."

We laugh again.

"I want you all to think. Who or what is fucking up your life? But I want you to think hard. Don't just pretend to think. I want you to struggle, have nightmares. I want God to show up, and I want you to talk to him. I want you to look at the person you see in the mirror, and talk to that person too."

María glances at me again. Or maybe not, maybe she's looking at all of us. But I can't help but feel like she's speaking to me, and the trembling has only increased, has spread throughout my whole body.

All through the weekend, I think about what María said. I review the things and people that could be poisoning us, but nothing stands out. Blasco and Moe go about their days as usual. Sometimes I feel like I'm living with extraterrestrials. They don't seem to understand our situation is critical.

Moe walks around the house with that indifferent look she's had for the last few months. It makes me think she's living in a dream state. There's Mom and her neuroses, Dad, absent as usual, school, everyone else, but none of it seems to touch her. We've been reduced to shadows.

Not long ago, she paid close attention to everything. If one of us was especially quiet, she'd draw something, write "I love you, Dad," or "I love you, Mom." If she got a bad grade, she would shut herself up in her room and study until she did better. That's how much she cared. Now, we could be bleeding out in the kitchen, and she'd probably just send a text to her group chat: "Parents," and the emoji that's rolling its eyes.

Sometimes I look at her phone, maybe I shouldn't, but I can't help it. Mostly there are selfies. She has an app where you can virtually try on clothes. They spend hours sending each other fake photos, glued to them as though they contain their entire lives.

And it dawns on me, while I'm snooping in Moe's phone. What Blasco and I need to do is release ourselves from our phones, from the iHome, from our personal computers.

I spend two days in ecstasy. I've finally found what's poisoning us, our lives will finally be complete.

I'm in such a good mood not even Blasco's pessimism can touch it. On Tuesday, it was all over the news. The charter for the Transnational Regional Bloc has been ratified. Apparently, the digital council will include international experts who will "make appropriate use of our data to lower crime rates and keep us safe." On the front page of the newspaper—it's amazing to get the paper again—there's a photo of the new intergovernmental organization, the president, a white woman, wears a stunning kimono-like trench coat. I wouldn't be surprised if they're suddenly all the rage, stylish but austere, completely congruent with the times—we need to shrink our egos, build greater awareness. The vice-president is a black man with an Afro and beautiful skin. It makes you feel good, seeing them.

If I could convince Blasco and Moe we have to cut back and be more aware, that'd be enough for me. I have to consult with María about how I should act with my family, Blasco has to stop being so negative, it's rubbing off on Moe.

In spite of the progress I've made through the week, on Friday, I wake up with the feeling I'm missing something again. What if getting rid of our phones and computers isn't enough? What if we need to dispose of something more essential? But what?

Dark clouds are gathering over me when a note from Momo arrives. She's invited María's entire group to the performance she's doing this Sunday. My spirits are lifted. We're finally part of something worthwhile. Everything is going to be just fine.

Angélica • Carlos • María

Now I wear a wig. It's wavy and brown, a little darker than my natural color, and it reaches past my shoulders. It's custom made, so there's no adhesive required, it stays on. To make sure it's clean and shiny, I use the spray that came with it once a week. I almost never take it off.

I keep my actual hair very short. Without the wig, I look like a man. Or a boy. Someone younger than me, shy.

I started wearing it two months ago. I found it in a catalog in September and knew the moment I saw it I had to have it. I'm done with the whole ordeal of hair, done attempting to smooth it, tying it back so tight to keep it from tangling I get a headache. Goodbye dye. Goodbye worrying about roots.

I wear the wig whether or not I go out.

If Lisa hadn't left me, I don't think I'd be wearing a wig. The morning after she casually told me she was in love, she said her work no longer inspired her, she needed something she could believe in, something "bigger than herself." Two days later, she disappeared.

By then, I had made two mistakes: first, I let Lisa see the notebook. I'm still not sure when that happened, probably I slipped up and left it out on my nightstand one night when she was over.

Second, I never figured out exactly what Hester's clues meant. But worse than that, I added my own section at the end. Without that section, Lisa would never have figured out what it was, or if she had, I could have at least defended myself. But that's not how it went.

Because it was Lisa who tipped off the clinic. There's no other explanation. I kept that notebook with me at all times. I was so paranoid by then that at work, I even carried it into the bathroom. I couldn't risk someone looking inside and getting suspicious, or accidentally recycling it—that's how worn-out it looked—and then I might never get it back.

It's likely that Lisa confessed in a one-on-one, we had them every two or three months to, as they said in our onboarding, "evaluate satisfaction and optimize resource allocation." They usually asked us about our colleagues. If we were comfortable, if there was anything we wanted to report. Maybe Lisa let slip that I hadn't been myself lately, said something about the notebook. Maybe that's why she cut off all contact.

Days after Lisa vanished, management at the Plant called me in for a special meeting. "We've confiscated your notebook. You understand the information you're tracking is confidential and therefore cannot circulate. We appreciate your tenacity and your dedication to science, however."

When the regional director, who had come out to our clinic just to meet with me, said those words, I knew it was the end. I took a sip of tea and steeled myself for whatever was coming. I was certain my firing was imminent, but instead of panic, I was gripped with a kind of euphoria, and for some reason I thought of pyromaniacs, how they must feel when they see their flames blotting out roofs, walls, and furniture.

The regional director also took a sip of tea and, smiling, said, "We've determined the best option for you is a change of scenery."

If they hadn't put me in charge of cloning and bone-marrow cryogenics, I wouldn't be looking at catalogs, nor would I be wearing a wig. There was a time when catalogs almost died out, when online shopping took hold, but they came back. I don't remember how I got interested in them again.

As a kid, I thought they were magical. Especially the ones from the grocery store. At first they were single sheets, just pages with coupons on them. Then, once I was living on my own, they turned into almost books, with glossy pages and that very specific scent. Actual books didn't smell like that, nor did any other printed item. Maybe it was the mixture of different kinds of ink, or the paper they used, or the warehouses that distributed them.

There was a time when you could spend an entire day reading catalogs. Furniture stores had them, hardware stores had them, computer stores had them. Clothing stores still sent them out even with online shopping. You could tell they didn't trust you'd go back to their websites, but assumed you'd keep the catalogs around.

That's where they put all their energy. Those early ones had stunning photos, beautiful men and women, beautiful clothes, pullout posters in vibrant colors, the large-format kind. A visual cornucopia.

I never loved going to the grocery store, and I didn't love boutiques either. I'd drop in every so often and buy just enough to replenish the unnecessary necessities. The Lisa period was the only time I enjoyed going to the store, just to be with her, to see how her expression changed when she found something she liked or something that surprised her, "that's challenging," she'd say, a sly smile on her face.

The point is, there was a time when catalogs all but disappeared. The Plant still put one out, and so did a few other specialty clinics. Those were different, though, printed on very thick paper, in faded blue ink, or dull gold, to give the impression of sumptuousness and calm. Sumptuousness and calm were what our clients—aspiring to the upper-class—were after. All the catalogs for cosmetic surgery clinics were almost identical, exclusive items strategically placed on the little waiting-room tables so the clients had something to entertain themselves with—actually, to sell the product, which wasn't so much a treatment, as they might have initially thought, but an idea. They paid for a new self-image, a better image, according to popular opinion.

Just like they now pay for the idea of being copied before their deaths, or uploading their minds to a hard drive, or something like that. No one claims it's possible—that's against company policy—but they infer and pay with their eyes closed. And because of that, and because antidepressants don't work for me, I've become obsessed with catalogs.

About three years ago, there was a renaissance. Online sales were down, though the companies denied it, withholding the data. All they were talking about in the news was climate change and the need for a regional governing body that could prevent immigration crises and protect us from new global threats.

The number of catalogs each consumer can access might be lower than it was pre-internet, but the quality of those catalogs is much higher. Their characteristic scent, part cheap ink, part fast food, has turned into something more neutral, like newly cut wood that's been treated with lye. That former scent some of us cherished is still detectable, if you look for it. Just a hint, in the background.

But it's not only the smell that has changed. Now they're more like books than ever, well bound, though perishable. After four or five months, their pages yellow, and they're dropped into recycling bins. The way they determine the contents has also changed. They're now adapted to each consumer, like internet ads, and that makes them desirable, almost collectors' items.

You don't get them automatically, like you used to. The company assesses your purchases, and at the end of three or four interactions—digital or in person, it's all recorded—they start sending your personalized catalog, with products an algorithm determines might be of interest to you.

At first, we didn't notice. But after a few months, when we went to friends' houses and compared—normally they're in the bathroom or some strategic spot in the living room—it was obvious. They were all different.

Yes, the differences are minor. Maybe yours doesn't have yellow products because they've deduced you don't like the color. It seems trivial, I know, but over time the differences add up, they become more profound. For example, yours has no mention of "lifestyle," they've noticed the word doesn't fit with your worldview, and other words show up instead. "Utility," "performance."

Today catalogs are so personalized that reading one is like reading yourself.

Since nothing burned and I'm wearing a wig and taking advice from catalogs, I ended up at a performance exhibition. The events magazine suggested it as the best birthday outing for me.

The theater is already buzzing when I get there, and like anyone who shows up at one of these things alone, I occupy myself with observation. Based on the clothing people are wearing, you can sort them into three groups. First, the ones corseted in outfits they've decided are appropriate for the theater, who probably got tickets last minute for a steal. They'll be disappointed and leave early, head to dinner. At dinner, they'll discuss the lack of quality contemporary theater.

Then there are the ones wearing clothes that don't seem to have been chosen for the occasion. They're in modest dresses with some detail or another that sets them apart from everyday clothing: a neckline cut lower than usual, sheer sleeves (the women) or matching sweaters and jackets (the men), fashioned in shinier fabric, in gold, vermillion, or dark-green shades suitable for late fall.

These ones get personalized catalogs. Not everyone does, the companies do the math and decide if their level of spending is worth the investment. This is also the group I belong to. It's unlikely the work will disappoint us. We come to shows like this often, we know they don't lead anywhere, but they're likelier to satisfy us than a day of frustrated shopping or one spent at home.

Finally, there are those who seem completely out of their element. Someone with extra tickets invited them, wanting to seem gracious. They're wearing jeans and sweaters, or—the women—wool dresses, garments more compatible with December or January weather, and they're going to get hot.

They're the only ones who will genuinely enjoy this. They'll think it was "haunting." Later, they'll call it "profound," will say it "turned everything upside-down." They'll sneak photos and describe the show to as many people as possible. They're going to feel as if they've had a once-in-a-lifetime experience.

I make an equal effort to avoid the members of all three groups, but a woman across the room keeps looking at me. There's still some time before the performance starts, but we're all here because the artist has them close the doors forty minutes early to build anticipation. It's an old trick and has lost its effect now that everyone knows about it: we're all just doing our best to kill time, enjoying hypercaloric, revivifying drinks. The woman is looking at me like she knows me, and that's when I realize. It's Lisa.

I look away immediately. I haven't seen Lisa since she disappeared from the Plant.

I barely recognize her. She's holding the hand of a kid who's probably ten or so. The event is family-friendly, the one thing that gave me pause when I went to buy my ticket. But you almost can't avoid that. There are so few children here that forbidding them entry would seem like a crime. And there's a new approach to parenting on the rise: "if it's good for you, it's good for your child," so now they're attached at the hip.

Out of the corner of my eye, I see Lisa looking at me again, but she seems unable to place me. It's the wig, it makes me look more sophisticated.

When I've calmed down and refocused on my glass of chardonnay—I drink wine because I don't want to live in fear of some cardiovascular event—I feel her hand on my shoulder.

"Angélica?"

Her hair is straightened and dyed lighter, not blonde, but a lighter brown. She looks much older than she should.

"You look amazing," she says.

The little boy is next to her, distracted by a cup of something bright pink.

"You look great too."

The things we shared crowd my mind: the pure scent her body gave off in the middle of the lab, the nights in my bedroom, caresses, but also how coldly she disappeared, how she betrayed me. There's no one else it could have been, I tell myself. I'd like her to disappear now. I feel the rejection I've clung to for years.

But she looks me straight in the eyes, and her look is bright and smiling.

I briefly try to return it, draw on a neutral smile. I want to make my excuses and go, but before I can, she asks, "So tell me. What are you doing now? Are you still at the Plant?"

"Yes, well, not in fertility. Now I'm in more of a consulting role."

Lisa laughs, and her laugh makes me think of her lightness, how easily she could adapt. "I knew you were going straight to the top, we all knew. You have that gift, that breadth of vision."

It's not so much her face that has aged, it's clear she's taken care of herself, she probably has access to all the midrange skin treatments. There's something else clouding her face.

"What about you?"

"I never got back on track. You know I wasn't doing well back then. So many highs, but also so many lows."

"So now what?"

"Now I take care of Ray. And I take care of myself. Now my job is to take care of everyone, the three of us, I mean. Someone has to, right?" She pauses briefly. "I take care of my husband, of course," she adds as if saying silly me, I forgot. "Yes, look, here he comes now. Great, I can introduce you."

Lisa adopts the right tone for casual social encounters. "I'm so glad we ran into each other. Call me sometime, OK? I'll give you my therapist's number. The things we do! We need to slow down, but if we slow down, then what?"

The husband is what I expected, you can tell from a distance he's in finance, probably an executive. He's in a tailored suit too formal for the event, and his face says everything's under control.

Before he gets to us, the boy lets go of Lisa's hand and runs to his father. The father dodges the hug his son was hoping for and high fives him, trying to show him how men do it, and that's when I realize it's Carlos.

These last eleven years have changed him too. There's no trace of his honey-colored hair, and his fully shaved head makes him look different, aggressive, less sweet than he seemed when I knew him.

He looks over at me, not for long, I guess he doesn't recognize me. He gives Lisa a totally neutral kiss, they're bored with each other. Then he looks at me another time, and I'm sure he knows who I am, but he says, "Ah, hi, nice to meet you."

I flail for a second then decide to play along. We talk about the Extraordinary Situation; we share funny stories from the lab. I was hilarious, Lisa says. It was really a special time. Carlos keeps sneaking looks at me. He's using that slightly mocking tone that came out when we joked around. Is it possible he knew Lisa and I were together when they met?

"We met in therapy, it was kismet." Lisa stresses these words and winks at me. "Sometimes the universe does come through, right?"

Lisa waits for me to be witty, to be who I was ten years ago, before the catalogs and the wig.

If anything about her was worth it, it's disappeared completely. The look in her eyes, all her gestures, I'm realizing now, remind me of a friend I had my last few years of college. She was average height, like Lisa, with eyes that same changeable green, different depending on the light or the color she was wearing, and she often put on a slight singsong voice. She looked like Lisa, but Lisa today—before, it had never occurred to me.

One day after the friend and I started our first jobs, mine at the Plant, hers at an import-export consultancy, we met up for drinks. She had just returned from Milan, where her suitcase had been stolen. She thought the whole thing was hilarious.

Apparently, her insurance covered baggage loss up to a shocking sum, this was before budget travel. She told them she'd packed some outrageously priced glasses, a designer dress or two, three pairs of designer shoes.

"With what insurance is giving me, I'm buying leather pants, real ones, don't tell me you don't think they're cool, and also the most expensive perfume I can find," she said, and cackled.

We met up again the week after, and indeed, she'd bought everything she said she would and more, she was exultant, though also jittery, as if spending all that money had made her adrenaline spike. "I feel drunk, and I haven't even had anything! Don't you love that?"

When I saw her again at our class reunion a few weeks later, she'd gotten lip filler. She kept covering her mouth with her hand, she felt uncomfortable. "I'm so superficial now," she said, winking.

In that moment, I felt bad for my friend, yet now, looking at Lisa, I'm almost nostalgic for Botox, for compulsive, absurd purchases. I'm nostalgic for a time when everything worked terribly but worked.

Completely miserable, my friend from college was happier than Lisa or I will ever be. She knew consumption was a placebo, but she also knew that it was enough to get her from one day to the next.

"Shall we, honey?" Lisa says.

When they've disappeared into the crowd—the room is huge, it could probably fit two or three hundred people—and I'm trying to process what just happened, why it happened, and what my life has turned into, another woman catches my attention.

She's an unusual type. She doesn't fit into any of my categories. Her clothing looks old and worn, it must have come from a thrift store. It's possible she's an artist, but her expression—highly focused, highly inquisitive—isn't one I associate with artists. Her face looks familiar, but more like an echo of someone I've known. Sometimes that happens to me—I see people I think I know, but I don't know them. There's just an echo inside them, a trace of someone else.

But this face, this face is too familiar, and when the chime sounds so you know the show is starting—I hate that tradition—I realize it's Mary, the VIP client, with her daughter, Ariadna. Carlos's daughter. In the moment right before they turn down the lights, I start to think things do work, but what's happened is, they now work in a way that leaves us out entirely. We're no longer puppets in the hands of economic powers, now there's another power, more profound, more astute. And it has nothing to do with us.

Carlos • Angélica • Diana

There's a wall a meter high in the middle of the room, and a lady climbs up on top of it. She's having a hard time, she's not as young as she used to be, she's not in great shape either. Finally, she makes it, huffing and puffing, drenched. We're so close we can see her sweat.

The thing is, once she does make it up on the wall, you think she's going to do something, don't ask me what—sing or talk, balance and walk end to end, but no, she just sits there, right on the edge of the wall, first looking down at the ground, then staring into space.

I'd give anything to be out for Sunday beers with the guys from work. These "performances" don't do it for me. But you can't say no to the woman who is the reason you're getting it up, especially not if that woman is your wife.

I don't know how much time the artist spends on the wall, but it feels like an eternity. When I'm sick to death of it, and my tie has started to strangle me because the heat is cranked all the way up, and the kids are running circles around the adults—the program states explicitly that minors are not to be reprimanded—the artist decides to move, she jumps down from the wall and then jumps from one side of it to the other.

"Jumps" is an overstatement, she's not agile enough for that, which makes the operation tough to watch. First she launches herself with her hands, then she wriggles up one knee, she tries to get her balance and sometimes slips and has to start from scratch. If she makes it, she stays put for a minute, just until she stops panting, then she gets down, she squeezes her hands together and lets herself drop. Frankly, it's unbearable.

But Lisa, my wife, loves it. Ever since Ray was born and she started doing yoga, meditation, reiki, all that shit, she's been obsessed with stuff like this. I'm a good sport, or I try to be. If it weren't for her and Diana, I would be totally impotent. And I probably would have been fired.

If I'm honest, I liked Lisa a lot more at the beginning, when she still had curly hair and was fucking Coach and a woman. I think our relationship peaked the day she showed me a photo and confirmed my sneaking feeling that the woman was Angélica. I was sleeping with a lesbian and screwing over my ex and Coach, all at the same time. In other words, I was cured.

It's too bad Lisa fell into my trap so fast. In less than a month, she decided she wasn't so into Angélica after all, and Coach had been fine and good, but she had no use for him anymore. At first everything was perfect, I was on a high, I loved that Coach was so suspicious, loved stabbing Angélica in the back. But then things got serious, and I got nervous. That's why I had to get back with Diana. I couldn't risk not being able to get it up again.

So we're here, drowning in bullshit, because there are women you can't say no to in life. If one of them offers you tickets, you accept them and take the other, because she "loves art."

After going up and down the goddamn wall several times, the "artist" falls flat on her face. Everyone saw that coming. Like I said, she's out of shape, she's too old to be doing this crap. They say she's the most influential living artist, her portfolio is stunning, et cetera. Maybe she should have paid more attention to her investment portfolio. Artists have it tough, we're not allowed to take them as clients, they're too stubborn, and anyway, it doesn't matter what they do, they have to keep working until they die, they're broke as shit.

When she falls, some people gasp. One woman screams, because she's not moving, and it'd be surprising if her skeleton were intact. But what do you know, after several minutes of maximum expectation—even the kids shut up—she stands and starts climbing the wall again.

If what the performance is trying to do is show us our lives aren't so bad after all, our trials are, in fact, minor, well, it's working. We're all going to feel stupendous once it ends and we're out getting air. It's like when Coach would make us pop in six, seven sticks of gum—the big ones, not those pitiful sugar-free chiclets—and chew and chew for minutes at a time. When he finally let us spit out the wad, the relief was so great our problems just disappeared, at least for a while.

At the end of five agonizing minutes, the artist falls again, and this time, she seems to have actually hurt herself. She's lying on the floor groaning. Is she faking it? Could be, but I don't think she's that good at acting. The audience holds their breath again, except for the kids, they've seen this movie before, they're not falling for it.

I'm starting to feel desperate. I'm hungry, it must be after three—a show before dinner is brutal, but people think only plebians go out at night now—and I'd kill for a beer. The lady is still on the ground, it seems like she'll be there a while. I start to think up exit strategies.

I locate Ray, he's a few rows back, showing another kid something on his phone. If I could get to him, I could convince him to tell Mommy he's dying of hunger, and Lisa would agree that we should go.

A man comes in through the doors at the back. He's tall, maybe late forties. No one moves a muscle. The man, seemingly oblivious to the surroundings, goes over to the artist and asks if she's OK.

The audience is still waiting with bated breath. Up until now, the artist hasn't opened her mouth, so everybody is wondering how she'll respond.

"No," she finally says. "I think I twisted my ankle."

The man nods, sucks his teeth, and says, "You're going to be just fine, let me get you some ice." He picks her up and transfers her to a chair I hadn't noticed.

"Thank you," she says. "I wasn't sure what to do."

"That's OK," the man replies. "Falling will do that. Just rest a minute, all right? We'll take care of this."

The man goes to the bar at the back, grabs a bag, fills it with ice, and returns to place it on her ankle.

She smiles for the first time, and the audience relaxes. Some people start to clap, but hardly anyone seconds the motion. No one applauds at these shows, another thing I find brutal. An ovation was always cathartic, a minute of magic, if the show had something going for it, and if not—more often the case—celebration that it was over, that we could leave.

"Well," says the man, "I'll be going now. You might want to get it checked out tomorrow, they'll probably give you a brace. Sprains heal quickly, though, you'll see."

The artist thanks the man, who disappears into the crowd. Then she gets back up. Guess the sprain must not be so bad. She looks at us, maybe a look of defiance—you see a lot of those these days—or maybe she's just deep in thought, and then she disappears right back through the door she came out of.

The audience starts to talk. This is the part I hate most. They say it was "incredible," that her medium is "consciousness itself"—"consciousness" is a buzzword—that she's "enlightened."

People also discuss the man's intervention. "Do you think it was rehearsed?"

"Impossible, it was too natural."

"He must be an artist too."

"Or a writer, or a philosopher."

"There are probably tons of philosophers here, these are *significant experiences,* performances are where the real art in this city is happening." The idea that he's a philosopher who ducked out because he's shy and didn't want to be cornered afterward spreads among the masses.

In less than fifteen minutes, it's taken as fact that the man was a scholar, a philosopher, and the work was brilliant and probed the depths of consciousness. There's euphoria in the room, so much so that I think if I slip out for a smoke, no one will notice.

On the way, I run into Diana, who is with Blasco. I furnish the necessary phrases, "unforgettable," "we're so lucky we had tickets," "what a gift," "thank you so much, Lisa's thrilled."

"Great for the kids, too, don't you think?" Diana replies.

Sometimes I can't tell if she's laughing at me, her husband, or everyone at the same time. Then I look at her and realize she isn't laughing at all, she's too busy maintaining her boss-wife exterior, her sheen of competence and power.

"Absolutely. They were into it. I bet you they never forget this."

Diana looks at me. She hates me a little, or if not that, she at least finds me annoying. I've never understood why she came back to me. Because she knew I couldn't say no? Because her husband is perfect for her, but boring? Because she turned him into her underling? Or maybe she really can't stand me, and that's what she likes.

More than once, she's told me off. "Is that how you talk to your clients?" But she knows the answer is yes, and that it works, and what we say we do is one thing, and what we have to do is another. It's a little routine she especially loves to put on in our monthly meetings, and then she'll slip me a note. She never uses email or text, she keeps all that very professional, and there we are again, her asking me for more, me giving in without knowing why, because I can't stand her either, because she's my boss, because I owe her, because she's buying, because I get hard when she scolds me.

"Go say hi to Lisa," I say. "She'd love to see you."

Diana says OK and she and Blasco go over to rub her nose in the fact that they're the ones who achieve things, not us.

I keep walking toward the exit, I'm already starting to see the light of late afternoon. I don't know how long we've been in here. It has to be after five and I'm starving. I can't figure out why no one is leaving, they must all live off air. Or maybe they're vegetarians, you lose your taste for real food and then you don't care if you eat or not.

Next to the exit is Ray, who waves at me. He's with Diana's daughter and another girl who looks like her. They're distracted with their phones. They look happy.

I guess it's good for kids to be with other kids, now that they're all only children.

As I'm heading toward the doors, I can hear their conversation.

"It's my turn," Diana's daughter says.

The other girl looks at her, furious. It must be a two-person game, so one person has to sit out.

"No," the other girl responds. "It's mine. You always try to cut."

"It's fine, guys," Ray says. He's always been soft, like his mother. "You can play, and I'll wait."

But Diana's daughter and the other girl have something else in mind. "Let's flip a coin," they say in unison.

They don't have coins, but they still call it that, it's just an app on their phones.

Diana's daughter wins, and the other girl simmers and waits. That's when I realize. They're flirting with Ray. And I feel a jab in my chest. Ray! Isn't he still just a kid?

I go out into the street, wanting to breathe, wanting fresh air, wanting to feel like I'm on solid ground instead of some slime that could swallow me any second.

It's cold as shit, too cold for November, or maybe it's just the contrast with the temperature inside. I light a cigarette. It's my last remaining vice. Quitting drinking was a breeze, relatively speaking. Lisa does nothing but hammer at me about smoking now. "You're killing your-self," "you must really care about us, huh," and every time she does, I feel the vice's roots deepening, it even answers for me, "what's the big deal," "would dying be so bad," "I'll quit when I want to."

So I breathe in, against everything.

"Every cigarette subtracts ten minutes from your life."

That's when I see him, the guy who helped the artist. He's wearing gray coveralls now, and carrying sacks of garbage through a gate near the building entrance.

The self-actualized philosopher is a maintenance man.

I hold the pack out for him, and he takes his place next to me on the wall.

"Thanks," he says. "It's good to take breaks, clear your head."

He goes on. "It's nice today, they could have brought the party out into the street. That's what I always say, it's too nice to keep people inside. But they don't listen. That's what happens, I guess, no one listens. We're all just going about our business."

"You work here all the time?"

"No, no, they have us on a rotation. They don't want us to get too used to any one place. Lowers productivity, they say."

I listen intently, nod so he'll keep talking. That's something they taught us in business school.

"But what does it matter if you get used to the place you're cleaning? I don't see why that would lower your productivity. At the end of the day, they check all the sites, and if yours isn't clean, you come back and you do it for free. But it's not really about the cleaning, it's about the conversation. They don't want us to stay in one place because they don't want us getting too friendly. These days just talking is basically a crime."

"Right," I say.

"So thank you, for your cigarette and your time. Take care now."

"See you later."

The maintenance man finishes loading his truck with sacks of garbage and pulls away.

For a minute I imagine others coming out and spotting the maintenance philosopher. That would have been pretty funny. Although they would probably just interpret it all as part of the show and go home doubly wowed by the final twist.

That would have been tragic, would have wrenched away the last little bit of will that's left in my chest.

You don't say no to the woman who's the reason you're getting it up, but when saying yes means you end up at a shit "performance" with the woman who made you go soft and the women who got you hard again, one of whom happens to be your boss, who you've been fucking for twelve years, then you notice your only son is already old enough to start dating, you realize that maybe at some point you should have thought about saying no.

María

They swarm to me like bees.

They think they're looking for the cure, the taste of honey. But what they really want is pain, for someone to confirm their worst suspicions about themselves, to deepen the wound. The wound is the only reason they carry on.

Data has run through my veins for so long that I can predict how they'll respond if I know how much they make, and I can figure out how much they make with one look at their clothes and their car. The human mind may be a mystery, but our behavior is predictable 95 percent of the time. All we need is the right data. Not empathy, just details, numbers, and then you can tell them whatever they want to hear.

I've successfully determined who are the most susceptible: middle-aged women with high-paying jobs and high levels of dissatisfaction. For them, I propose weekly sessions; they come religiously for their fix.

Once installed in your system, the data is like a cancer, growing inside you, rebuilding you. So now I have two bodies, one of mere flesh and blood, the other of data, invisible and expanding.

Each new visitor brings more data that feeds my second body: the perfume they wear, the opinion on organic food generally held by those in the third-highest income bracket (it's been proven that the health benefits are minimal, but the environmental benefits are significant), the most popular place to vacation in the countryside. Only middle-income families go to the beach now, the ones who didn't sell properties when they should have, or haven't adjusted to the times and still associate the ocean with the release of a vacation. The UV risks are higher on the coast, you should stay away, or at least that's what the others think, in the higher-than-average income brackets, they got rid of their beach houses at the right time—they had good financial advisors who forecast it all, who kept an eye on investment trends—and now they just go to the countryside.

I don't need to be connected. Once the data is in your system, everything feeds it.

When Ariadna was born, I thought I would finally escape. I logged out of every database, stopped using the internet, and for a while, I did feel free. Around that time, we came out here and started to "counsel." At first, I didn't notice. I truly believed I had gotten out.

But before Ariadna's first birthday, I came to understand that it was impossible. It happened one afternoon, when were out walking through nearby cornfields.

It was hot, summer had just begun, Ariadna was already combining her first syllables—she's always been precocious—and was obsessed with repeating them over and over. The words didn't mean anything, she repeated them just to hear the sound of her voice.

That's what I wanted, too: my own voice.

The fact that Ariadna was finding hers gave me hope. Everything seemed possible in that moment.

Then a man showed up, running along the same path. He was covered head to toe in high-end gear, which at that time was very fashionable: a tight black shirt with fluorescent-orange sleeves, black and fluorescent-green Lycra pants, and shoes that were three different colors. He was running fast, almost sprinting. The path was narrow, I had to move Ariadna's stroller off to one side. We almost fell in a ditch.

I was furious, and that activated the data in my body: here's your typical privileged guy, he left his wife and is training like this to impress his much younger lover. Now that he's paying alimony, there's not much left to cover her whims: she's an assistant at his office, she doesn't make nearly as much as he does. So he's invited her for a weekend away in the countryside, where there's a family house he's ignored for last few years.

I didn't get a single detail wrong.

The man was divorced, and for a while, he would strut around the village with his girlfriend like he owned it. A few months later, he stopped coming, in part, I guess, because his lover (platinum-blonde, prone to cellulite) found it boring, and in part because the locals started giving him dirty looks. It had bothered me so much, his entitlement, his hideous outfit, the carelessness with which he'd almost trampled Ariadna, that I'd decided to spread a rumor—I made a fake social media profile—that his wife had left him because he'd abused her for years. It's incredible how quickly fake news spreads, and how easily people believe you, if you're using the right tools.

So, you could say I won. But I also lost everything.

My own voice, if I'd ever had one, or even a chance at one, was gone. All we had was Ariadna's voice.

From that day on, I devoted myself to building my daughter a chance at a voice.

I like to think of myself as a sex worker whose only child is attending a fancy boarding school.

So Ariadna can have her own voice, I prostitute myself.

Starting was easier than I thought it would be. I weaned myself off the digital world, at least outwardly, and left a trail of breadcrumbs between me and the people who needed me.

"A former major player in the world of big data, she disappeared to raise her daughter in nature."

"'We're living in a toxic society, we need to reconnect with our deeper selves,' says María Lebrel, the data scientist who renounced technology."

"The scientist, one of the most renowned of her generation, now offers counseling to a select group in her mountain home."

Two or three planted articles, that was enough. The rest took care of itself. They started to come, like rats drawn by the Pied Piper.

They always want more. More suffering, more guilt, more rejection, higher fees.

And that's how we keep Ariadna at this school of our own creation, far from data, far from its assault on human consciousness. Here, Ariadna is safe, and her mind can grow.

We harvest the fruits of the earth. We don't consume anything we haven't grown ourselves or watched someone else grow. We don't mind killing chickens, defeathering them, and eating them, if they're our chickens, but under no circumstance will we consume food that is packaged or canned. We're uncompromising there. You never know what a chicken might contain, or a yogurt, a jar of jam. You never know which transaction will sink you right back in the data heap.

Ariadna is part of me, but she's stronger, and I know she's going to make it. I know it.